Last Summer in Agatha

Last Summer in Agatha

KATHERINE HOLUBITSKY

ORCA BOOK PUBLISHERS

Canadian Cataloguing in Publication Data
Holubitsky, Katherine, 1955 –
Last summer in Agatha

ISBN 1-55143-188-2 (bound); 1-55143-190-4 (pbk.)

I. Title.
PS8565.O645L36 2001   jC813'.54   C2001-910203-8
PZ7.H74279La 2001

First published in the United States, 2001

Library of Congress Catalog Card Number: 2001087479

Orca Book Publishers gratefully acknowledges the support of our publishing programs provided by the following agencies: the Department of Canadian Heritage, The Canada Council for the Arts, and the British Columbia Arts Council.

Cover design by Christine Toller
Cover illustration by Don Kilby
Printed in Canada

IN CANADA	IN THE UNITED STATES
Orca Book Publishers	Orca Book Publishers
PO Box 5626, Station B	PO Box 468
Victoria, BC Canada	Custer, WA USA
V8R 6S4	98240-0468

03 02 01 • 5 4 3 2 1

For Linda

Acknowledgements:

My sincere thanks goes to the following people: to
Bob Tyrrell for his insight and invaluable suggestions
during the development of the manuscript; to
Dr. Melissa Ochotsky, who shared her remarkable
knowledge and experiences working with horses, and
to the entire staff of Centre High School, Edmonton,
for the support and encouragement they provide the
young people who inspire me everyday.

ONE

The mouth of the cave was a dark patch on the sandstone bluff. It sat at the edge of O'Conner's ranch just before the flat yellow land slid into Buffalo Coulee. The cave was cool inside, even in the still heat of summer, when the air was suffocating and the only creatures that moved dragged their bellies close to the ground.

We'd reach the cave by walking west from Agatha past the exhibition grounds. Then we'd trek half a mile along the railroad tracks through the sagebrush and prickly pear cactus. Giant grasshoppers kicked up by our sandals left sticky brown smudges where they smacked into our bare arms. I'd wipe the spit off with the corner of my T-shirt. And almost always I'd have to twist my hair up off my sweaty neck. I was just not used to the bold sun and scorched ground.

A train trestle crossed the river several hundred feet down from Buffalo Coulee. If we were in the cave around eleven o'clock in the morning, we'd often spot Rib Bone Squire cross it on his way into town. His wild white hair trailed out behind him like an abandoned old magpie nest.

"Don't move or he'll see us," my friend Anna told me the first time I saw him.

"Who is he?"

"Rib Bone Squire. He lives in a shack on Rasmussen's land on the other side of the river. He's a cold-blooded killer."

Michael rolled his eyes and guffawed. He came over to where we cringed in the shadows.

"You still believe that old story? The guy's harmless. He's a hermit. That's all."

Anna ignored him. "When they were eight years old, Mrs. MacPherson's twin sister disappeared down here by the river. Six months later her bones were dug up, picked cleaner than if vultures had done it. Right in Rib Bone's back yard."

"The bones were half a mile away and that was twenty-five years ago. They never found the killer or anyone else to blame. Dad said Squire was a loner and a sitting target."

Michael made sense. Still, whenever I saw Rib Bone cross the train trestle, I didn't move.

Long before I arrived in Agatha, Michael and his friend Scott had raised posts, then wedged three beams across them to strengthen the ceiling of the cave. They had hammered timbers against the walls. They had widened a crack in the earth above the cave to create a skylight. Through this, a block of prairie sunshine stretched across the floor. Michael told me the skylight had grown since they'd dug it. When I asked him how it had grown, he'd smiled and shrugged as if it were magic. But when a train rumbled by, he'd pointed to the skylight and the handful of earth crumbling quietly to the floor.

Michael and Scott had dragged an old cattle trough down to the cave and positioned it beneath the skylight to catch run-off. They had brought a battered old coffee table from home. They had built chairs from the discarded fencing that Mr. O'Conner left stacked for them in one corner of his field.

By the time I met Michael last summer, he didn't actually spend much time in the cave anymore. But he still liked to wander down to it once in a while. Sometimes we'd just sit in the mouth of the cave and watch pelicans circle high above the South Saskatchewan River. Or we'd look across to the powdery white bluffs which were riddled with bank swallow holes.

Anna told me it was Michael and Scott's cave. It had *always* been their cave. "Even though," she'd said, "Cory Sparks and his friends have tried about a million times to kick them out."

One of those times was a month before I'd gone to Agatha. Cory had dropped a wasp nest through the skylight while Michael and Scott were playing cards during lunch hour. Scott had cleared out fast but Michael didn't make it. He was allergic and when he got stung

3

he'd swelled up like a plump white mushroom. His mom was livid and called the principal of the school.

■ ■ ■

I had gone to southern Alberta to stay with my Uncle Colin and Aunt Sandy for the summer. Two weeks earlier, at the beginning of June, my brother, Sean, had packed his saxophone and left for the Berklee School of Music in Boston. My dad is an engineer with an oil company where we live in Vancouver, but quite often — actually, most of the spring — he worked out of town.

I missed Sean. For about an hour. Until I realized that life was sweet! The computer was now all mine. Three days after he left, I was humming happily, stepping lightly up the stairs, when Dad stopped me.

"Rachel," he said. "I've got a special surprise for you."

"Oh yeah?" I continued humming.

"I've got a job in Yellowknife for July and August, and since you and Mom are both on holidays for the summer, I thought it would be fun for the two of you to tag along. How about it?"

Panic paralyzed my face so that I quit humming. I looked at Mom, who turned from the newspaper and gave me her best let's-try-a-little-positive-thinking teacher's smile.

"You'll love it, dear. We'll think of it as an adventure."

An adventure? Being alone in a hotel room with my parents for two months? It would be more of an adventure to spend the summer watching golf on TV.

Still, it had been put as a question. I considered the idea for five seconds.

"Thanks. But I think not. I'll just stay home."

Mom and Dad looked at one another.

"Look, if you think about it, I'll be doing you a favor if I don't go."

Dad frowned. "How?"

"I can bring in the mail and cut the grass, and I'll have my friends stay over to make it look like someone is actually living here."

Dad frowned harder.

I shouldn't have mentioned the friends staying over thing. Mostly because Dad didn't like my friends. At least, he didn't like one of them. He didn't like Troy Atkinson, which he made pretty obvious by the scowl on his face whenever Troy phoned. Troy was two years older than me and I'd sort of been going out with him for a couple of months. Dad didn't like him *because* he was older than me, because more than once he'd seen him hanging around outside the video arcade during school hours, and because, well, "he's a half-naked layabout on the fast track to nowhere" were his actual words.

I hardly think that just because a person wears a muscle shirt it qualifies him as being half-naked, although, and I would never admit it to Dad, the layabout part was beginning to fit. Troy hadn't called me since I'd told him I wanted to start doing things other than watch the same old re-runs of *The Dukes of Hazzard*.

"Yeah, like what?"

"Well, maybe we could ride our bikes around Stanley Park?"

"Why?" He was looking at me like I'd suggested we crawl across the Gobi Desert.

"For something different."

"And what if we're not back by four?"

"Why do we have to be back so early?"

Troy frowned. "Don't *The Dukes of Hazzard* mean *anything* to you?"

Geez, you'd think suggesting a bike ride was some huge insult!

My friend, Leslie, says I'm too picky. "So, he likes cars. What's wrong with that?"

"It's not the fact that he likes them. It's the way he likes them. Sitting on the couch, laughing hysterically when the General Lee screeches around another corner."

"Yeah — and?"

"And — it's not interesting and it's not funny!"

Leslie threw her hands in the air. "I don't get it. Why do you need interesting when he's so great looking?"

Leslie was absolutely right. She didn't get it!

"Come on, Dad. I'm almost sixteen. I can cope."

And for one very brief millisecond, Mom looked as if I might have got her thinking. But, as with most things I'd suggested over the course of the spring, Dad's reaction was lightning fast.

"Forget it. The answer is definitely, absolutely, no!

You're coming to Yellowknife." He sat down, pushed back his glasses and began reading.

Ooh — what was with him lately? I pounded as hard as I could up the stairs.

Things were pretty tense around our house for the next week; I'd guess the total number of words exchanged between Dad and me to be somewhere around ten. But then Aunt Sandy called and invited me to spend the summer in Alberta. She and Uncle Colin are both veterinarians, and she asked if I would like to help them in their clinic. I considered it; the clinic would be fun, but dead and dusty Agatha? I wanted things to *happen* this summer. What were the chances of anything ever happening there? I looked at Mom, who was sitting at the kitchen table, frowning over a crossword puzzle. I looked at Dad. His face was all serious as he scraped the burnt bits off his toast. I thought about Leslie and how she was spending all of July at swim camp. On second thought — what was holding me here?

"Yes!" I'd blurted into Aunt Sandy's ear.

I think she'd pulled back from the phone because it was a few seconds before she replied with, "Good, we'll look forward to it then."

■ ■ ■

I met Scott Cardinal the day after I arrived in Agatha. He was pushing a lawn mower down the street across from Aunt Sandy's house. I was kneeling on the sidewalk, trying to get the chain back on her century-old bike. I was trying to fit all the greasy little gears in the sprockets, and up to that point, I had not been very successful. Huh! Thinking I had finally done it, I threw a leg over the bike and began riding down the road. The gears ground and clanked as they sprang from the sprockets — again. If there was only a garage on the corner like in any normal place, I could just *pay* someone to do it for me. But this was not a normal place and there was only one Shell station and it was out on the highway. I flopped down on the grass to think up a new plan.

"Need some help?" I glanced up to see Scott, grinning, with his hand held toward me. Anna had already filled me in on who he was. In fact, in one night she had filled me in on almost every living being in Agatha. Although I still don't know how she found out some of the personal stuff. Anyway, she'd said that Scott was cool. She'd also told me that *nothing* was going to get in the way of him becoming an architect.

"A sad fact," she had sighed, pulling her knees to her chest. She'd then looked dreamily out her bedroom window and I figured that *nothing* included Anna Klaus.

I took Scott's hand and he hauled me to my feet. On the way up, I noticed that his grip was strong, his hand was callused and his watch was spotted with green paint. Once on my feet, I noticed a little more. His T-shirt was ripped, the knees of his jeans were worn to a clump of strings, and the dark hair poking out from beneath his baseball cap was shedding yellow dust. I was pretty sure that I hadn't caught him on one of his better days.

"Is something wrong?"

Oops. I guess I'd been checking out the yellow dust a little too long. I realized I'd also stepped back a bit. *Well*, what if it was a symptom of some weird, contagious disease only known in these parts?

"Uh, no, it's just that —" It was impossible to ignore it, "— you seem to have dust or something in your hair."

"Oh." He pulled off his baseball cap and smacked it against his leg. He brushed the dust from his hair and rubbed it out of his eyebrows. "It's sawdust. I've been working. Better?"

I nodded.

"Good. I wouldn't want you to think I have some horrible disease."

I smiled weakly.

Scott only laughed. He clapped his hat back on his head, lifted Aunt Sandy's bike off the road and squatted next to it on the ground.

"Now, you hold the bike and I'll get this thing back on."

So that is what we did. Two minutes later the chain was on and Scott was testing it, rolling the bike back and forth. While he wiped his hands on the rag Aunt Sandy had given me, he nodded toward her house.

"You know Doctors Bennett and Hefferman?"

"They're my aunt and uncle. I'm staying with them for the summer. I'm Rachel Bennett."

He smiled again, introduced himself, and told me he lived across the street. He also told me he was sixteen and that he was building fences at Armstrong's Stables for the summer. He then asked me if he could show me around Agatha. When I didn't answer right away, he shrugged.

"It will only take thirty minutes. And that's if I give you the extended tour."

At that very moment a screen door slammed. Two doors down, Anna stepped onto her front porch. She wore white clamdiggers, a navy halter top and her long sandy hair was swept up. Planting her hands on her hips, she peered at us over miniature sunglasses.

"Actually, I was about to meet Anna."

Anna Klaus was two months older than me and had lived all her life in Agatha. Besides knowing everybody and everything, she also worked at the clinic, where she'd been helping Uncle Colin and Aunt Sandy since she was ten. Anna jumped from the porch, swung her bike from around the side of the house and sailed toward us.

"I see you've discovered Rachel." She made circles around Scott. "Coming with us?"

He looked at me. "You don't mind?"

When I told him of course I didn't mind, Scott wheeled the lawn mower up to his house and disappeared into the garage. Seconds later, he soared down the driveway and across the road on his own bike. He skidded to a stop next to Anna. "Ready?"

I looked at the two of them with their feet strapped

to shiny pedals, polished mountain bikes shimmering in the sun, revved up, waiting for me. I sighed and climbed onto Aunt Sandy's rusted-out heap. It creaked and complained until I wanted to tell it to quit it. I faced Anna and Scott. Without much enthusiasm, I replied, "Ready."

They both began laughing.

"Hey, you should be nice to me. I'm a visitor here."

So with Scott in the lead and Anna beside him, and me rattling behind them, we rode the six blocks to the center of town. Once we had turned on to Broadway, we cruised past *The Agatha Bulletin,* MacPherson's Drug Store, and a parade of clapboard storefronts that reminded me of an old western movie set. We passed by Potter's Shoes, Black's Hardware, a Sears order office, the Roxy Theatre and the new brick library. We crossed the street in front of Ferguson's Fish and Chip Shop. We rode through Rotary Park, past the white gazebo, and along the river and across the railroad tracks and all through the neighborhoods on the other side. It did only take thirty minutes. Give or take a few. Even when we figured in the time it took to buy a raspberry slush at Dot's Diner. And the stops we had to make to coax my dying bike to go on.

Then Anna suggested that we ride up to the exhibition grounds. Once again we crossed the railroad yard that split Agatha. We were coasting along next to the old train station when we bumped into Michael Bell.

Michael's bike was lying on the sidewalk, and *he* was hanging from the top of the twelve-foot steel mesh fence, watching what was happening with the trains in the railway yard. Anna and I cringed at the screech and bang of coupling cars.

"That is so cool!" Michael cried when the clanging had stopped. He sprang to the sidewalk, leaving the steel fence chattering behind him. "Hi," he said when he landed, which was also the first time he noticed me. "I'm Michael. Who are you?"

"This is Rachel," said Anna, pointing a finger at me like I was a picture in the school yearbook.

"Oh," Michael glanced at Anna and then at me, like I might have something wrong with my tongue. "Hi, Rachel. Where are you from?"

"She's from Vancouver. She's staying with Dr. Bennett for the summer. He's her uncle and she's going to be working in the —" Anna stopped mid-sentence, because I butted in.

"I'm going to be working in the clinic."

I wanted him to *know* there was nothing wrong with me because he was easily the most interesting part of the tour so far.

Michael laughed.

Anna only smiled a little, climbed on her bike and started after Scott, who was now halfway up Exhibition Road.

"Come with us," she called back. "We're riding up to the exhibition grounds."

Michael answered with a wave of his hand. But neither of us made a move to follow. He smiled at me.

"So — you like trains?" I asked, using my uncanny ability to state the obvious when I don't know what else to say. I motioned toward the railway yard.

He didn't answer my question right away, and when I looked back to see why he hadn't answered, I saw that he was checking me out.

"Yeah," he said, "I like trains. Among a lot of other things."

I didn't ask about the other things. Instead, I began pushing my bike along the road. Michael picked up his own bike and wheeled next to me. He was quiet again, but this time it was Aunt Sandy's bike he was checking out.

"Where did you find that antique?"

"My aunt pulled it down from the rafters in her garage."

Throwing a leg over the frame, I started to pedal. The old bike groaned again.

Michael grimaced. "Oh man, that's brutal! Here, let me ride it for a while. You take mine."

I stopped. I looked at his very new, very amazing Schwinn. I looked at him. He was smiling a little, but he seemed to be serious about trading bikes.

"Really?"

"Of course, really. "

What a thoughtful guy! We made the switch.

Michael pulled a hand through his curly black hair, bent down and made a few adjustments to the bike. He hopped on and rode along next to me. He asked me why I had come to Agatha. He wanted to know what kind of plane I'd flown in from Vancouver to Calgary. I had no idea, but when he suggested it, I told him it was possible it had been a 737, although I couldn't tell him if the engines had been on the wings. Yes, there had been quite a bit of turbulence. And yes, the flight had been too short for a movie. Yes, I had seen *Alien*. No, I had not seen *The Relic*.

"Well, don't bother," he told me, "It's a rip-off of *Alien*. What about *Alien III*? Have you seen that?"

"Hey," I laughed, no longer caring what I said because Michael was so easy to talk to. "I think it's my turn to ask you a couple of things."

He was going into Grade 11. He was working as a handyman at Goodwyn's Wildlife Rehabilitation Farm for the summer and he lived with his mom and dad. No, he didn't have any brothers or sisters. He collected old horror movies and it was too bad he didn't know about me coming because he would have asked me to look for the collector's edition of *Army of Darkness*. Oh well, I would do it as soon as I got back. Yes, he owned a pair of cowboy boots and a Stetson. He even had a set of pistols. He got them for his birthday one year.

"Really? Pistols?"

"Yup. I even have the sheriff's badge, but I haven't worn it since the silver paper peeled off the cardboard when Scott sprayed me with a hose in '91. We were six."

When I laughed at what an idiot I was, Michael smiled. And I guess, looking back, that was probably the first clue I had that something was wrong. It was Michael's smile. It was a friendly smile, his dark eyes sparkled and it looked really good on him, but it was the way one corner of his mouth stayed where it was that wasn't quite right. Like whatever tugged at him inside kept that one corner of his mouth pulled down.

"Come on," he said, racing ahead of me. He called back, "I'll meet you at the top." And he took off faster than I could go. I watched him grind that old bicycle until he passed Anna and Scott and disappeared around a bend in the road at the top of the hill.

I'd known Michael five minutes and already I knew I really liked him. He had not only traded bikes with me, which was a pretty thoughtful thing to do, but I'd also never seen anyone get so excited just watching a bunch of noisy old trains. Or anyone work so hard to ride a worthless, rusted-out bike to the top of a hill.

■ ■ ■

I wasn't sure why Anna figured the exhibition grounds were worth the trek up. There was nothing there but a deserted racetrack and empty bleachers and a whole lot of naked brown field. Standing beneath the sign, "Agatha Rodeo and Exhibition, August 18-20," Anna pointed to some bare spots on the scruffy ground.

"That's where the midway is set up. The casino goes there. The coin toss and fishing hole over there. And —"

"Potter ropes that area on the other side of the pavilion off for fireworks," cut in Scott. He must have seen my eyelids slipping because he finished with, "And, I guess that's about it." He lifted his baseball cap, swept his hair back and clapped it on again.

"Unless she wants to see your cave."

"You have your own cave?"

"Yeah, we have our own cave. Doesn't everybody?" Michael laughed. He and Scott parked their bikes next to the fence. "We'll leave our bikes here. Come on."

Anna and I also parked our bikes and we followed the railroad track out of town.

The air was still and the sun was hot and a massive blue sky swept over and around us and beneath us. We hopped from tie to tie. We balanced on the rails, kicking gravel, breathing in the thick smell of creosote. Steadied by Michael's hand, I climbed up onto the top rail of a fence where he told me if I looked real hard I could see the Sweet Grass Hills of Montana. Squinting a hundred miles into the distance, I could see them, a soft purple swell where the land met the sky. I looked back to where Scott and Anna were tossing dry old cow pies at each other across the field.

"That is so gross! How can you guys even touch that stuff? Hey!" I jumped from the fence and ran with the air in my face when they turned and threw them at me.

We reached the end of O'Conner's land where we left the track, hopped the fallen fenceposts and followed the trampled path as it curved down a slope and around the side of a hill. I stood next to Anna, peering into the mouth of the cave. It was dim at first after the white light we'd been walking in, and musty smelling. I blinked several times before the shapes inside began to make any sense. There were two people in the cave.

Swinging a bucket of red paint from one hand, Cory Sparks had blond spiky hair and he stood with his back to us. With his free hand, he was painting graffiti all over the wall. He turned when he heard us. After looking briefly at Anna and Scott and Michael, his eyes stalled on me. It got a little uncomfortable, so I was thankful when Michael moved to my side. Cory turned his back to us again. The words next to what-ever warped message he was working on read, "Eat dirrt, Cardinal."

"Thought you needed some cave art to brighten the place up," Cory continued painting. "Who's she?"

Anna fussed and fumed and told him I was of no interest and wasn't he just a tad old for that kind of stuff and when was he going to grow up.

I looked at her. I was of no interest? She could maybe have used another term.

Taylor Sparshatt laughed. He was short and squat and he fit so tightly into one of the wooden chairs that I thought he might be stuck. It made a splintering noise as he leaned back in it. "Yeah, but there's not much to look at in here."

Scott and Michael nailed him with a look. I wasn't

sure if it was because of the painting or because Taylor had cracked their chair. Anyway, the reason wasn't important because at that point I was thinking about slinking out and returning to the fairgrounds for my bike, not really knowing any of them or how far this could go. I remembered the one fight my brother Sean had been in — at least, the one that I knew about. I was sitting in the kitchen when he'd walked in the door. His nose was slightly twisted and blood was dripping down his shirt. It had not been a pretty sight and all I knew was that I didn't want to see anything like it again.

But Scott only folded his arms and leaned back against the wall of the cave. "And that's the best you could do? Looks more like Taylor's little sister did it. In fact, maybe you should bring her down here to check out your spelling. This might come as a shock, but the word dirt only has one 'r'."

That made Cory stand back from the wall and examine the letters. Annoyed, he muttered something to Taylor. Taylor shrugged. Cory set the bucket down and put a line through one of the "r"s.

While he was doing it, Michael sprang forward and swept up the bucket of paint. He then drew back, threatening to toss it at Cory, who backed slowly against the wall of the cave.

"All right, Sparks. You and Sparshatt get lost."

Cory remained where he was, but Taylor stood up and began moving toward Michael like he was ready to fight.

"One more step, Sparshatt, and I'll turn you into a Christmas ornament."

Taylor hesitated. "You're bluffing."

"Oh, yeah? Try me. Come on, one step."

At that point, I let out a little laugh. Because when I thought about it, the whole scene was actually quite funny; Michael standing there, threatening to coat them in crimson. Cory and Taylor not moving, like the paint can was something much more sinister, like a gun.

So I was kind of surprised when no one else was smiling. Finally, Cory lifted a hand and without saying anything else, he and Taylor left the cave.

I stared after them. I wondered if maybe I'd missed something.

"That was easy," I whispered to Anna. "I mean, I'm sure he would never have actually done it."

"Michael?" Anna turned to me. "Oh yeah, he'd do it. He'd do it in a second."

She said it like it had happened before.

Once Cory and Taylor were gone, Scott found a piece of board in the grass outside and while he used it to scrape away Cory's cave art, Anna smoothed out the dirt below the wall. I helped Michael by holding the chair steady while he pounded it back together with a rock.

"Come on," he said, when we were finished. "We'll come back another time."

We walked back along the railroad tracks. For the first ten minutes, Anna complained about Cory and

Taylor. Michael and Scott said nothing for awhile. But then they started a game of soccer with a tumbleweed, and Michael suggested we push over a sleeping cow.

Anna told him to stop being so juvenile.

"All right. I'll push you over instead." Michael took off after Anna, who tore down the tracks as fast as she could go. She stopped when she stepped smack in the middle of a soft wet cow pie.

"Michael!"

Scott and Michael almost fell down laughing. And they continued laughing all the way to the exhibition grounds. So by the time we got home I really didn't think that Cory's messing up their cave bothered them. But that was before I knew about Nick and what had happened. It was before I knew why everyone had taken Michael so seriously. It was before I knew how close to the edge he really was.

TWO

Every second Friday, Uncle Colin drove out to Goodwyn's Wildlife Rehabilitation Farm, west of Agatha. He would tend to the sick and injured animals, taping up broken wings and stitching torn hides. The first Friday I was in Agatha, he asked Anna and me if we would like to come along.

I told him I'd like to. It sounded like it could be fun — in a laid-back, countryish sort of way. I imagined there would probably be a couple of big friendly dogs to pat and maybe a doe-eyed cow. It would just stand there munching on sweet-smelling hay while we milked it. I'd seen it on TV.

And — there was also the fact that Michael worked there.

Uncle Colin tossed his farm kit in the jeep, we all hopped in and we drove down Broadway and up Rundle Road, which took us out of Agatha. Once we were on the highway, there was not a single bump or swell as far as you could see. Uncle Colin told us that over the years the Goodwyns had nursed hundreds of animals — hawks, antelope and even rattlesnakes — back to health, any wild animal that was lucky enough to have been found after injuring itself and left in their care. Earlier that week, a farmer had brought them a fox that had become dehydrated after being caught in a skunk trap. Uncle Colin also had to vaccinate twenty head of cattle.

The farm was ten miles past Rasmussen's ranch on Highway 1. We drove past brown-eyed Susans and buffalo berries growing wild in the ditches. We drove past a muddy slough where Uncle Colin pointed to the purple loosestrife struggling to take hold. We were driving past Rasmussen's ranch when I noticed Anna sit up. She was scanning the land that stretched from Rasmussen's farmhouse down toward Buffalo Coulee, like she was looking for something. She saw me watching her.

"Megan Gillis is missing," she explained.

"Oh." I searched with her. "Who is Megan Gillis?"

She shrugged. "Someone from school. Scott figures she's run back to her dad's in Calgary again. She fights with her mom all the time. I don't believe it though."

"Why?"

"It's too simple."

"Where do *you* think she is?"

"Dead."

"Dead?"

"Uh-huh. Rib Bone Squire got her. Just like he got Mrs. MacPherson's sister."

Uncle Colin looked amused. He smiled at Anna in the rearview mirror. "You mean *Richard* Squire. Who, by the way, Rachel, despite the wild stories," he winked at Anna, "is a very gracious man."

"Yeah, well, whatever."

"What makes you so sure? I mean, if she's run away to her dad's before?"

"It's *so-o* obvious. He set it up. He picked her because everyone would think that she'd taken off to Calgary. Nobody would look too hard. Not for a while anyway, until the evidence was well covered up."

Uncle Colin was laughing.

"Anna," he said, "Stephen King has nothing on you."

We turned off the highway and drove down the gravel lane that led to Goodwyn's farmhouse. Michael was riding a tractor, cutting the grass next to the pond. He waved. Once Uncle Colin had parked in front of the old gray barn, we stepped from the jeep and breathed in the heavy sweet smell of freshly cut grass.

Mrs. Goodwyn appeared in the doorway, said hello quickly, and rushed Uncle Colin inside. A neighboring rancher had just brought in a fawn that had been hit by a truck earlier in the morning. Not wanting to put added stress on the animal by crowding around it, Anna and I stayed outside.

Anna led me through the garden where the sunflowers were already the size of pie plates. She introduced me to two permanent residents: a three-legged coyote and a bald eagle with only one eye. She taught me how to ride a donkey across the farmyard, although she neglected to teach me the part about what you should do if they try to sweep you off their back by cramming beneath the low branches of a crabapple tree. Which mine did. The miserable little beast. And Anna, my so-called friend, didn't even try to stop him; she just stood there laughing and watched it come.

On our way back to the barn, we spotted Mr. Goodwyn standing in the far corner of the barnyard. He was inspecting the gate that led to the back field. He waved us over.

"Girls, I could use your help over here."

Wondering how *I* could possibly be of any use to him, I followed Anna as she weaved around cattle, leapt over cow pies and plodded through muck to reach him. Anna introduced us.

"Boomerang broke through the gate again," he told us. "If he had a choice, he'd rather be in the back field. But I can't let him back there until we repair the fence on the other side of the creek. I need you girls to help me get these cattle in the barn. That'll make the vaccinating go faster for Dr. Bennett."

"No problem," we said.

Well, actually, Anna said it. I only nodded, because at that point, I wasn't quite sure if getting the cattle in the barn would be a problem or not.

Anna and Mr. Goodwyn came up with the plan.

They would shoo the cattle toward the barn door and I would block their path so that they didn't plow through the broken gate.

"All right," I nodded agreeably to what Mr. Goodwyn said. But as soon as I thought he was out of earshot, I whispered to Anna, "How exactly am I supposed to do that?"

"Just stand there."

"Just stand here? What difference is that going to make?"

Mr. Goodwyn overheard me. "Don't look so worried. If they go for the gate, they'll turn when they see you." He winked at Anna. "At least traditionally that's what they've done."

Traditionally?

"The important thing to remember is that they're afraid of you."

I looked at Boomerang, who was at least a thousand pounds heavier than me. If Boomerang *really* wanted to get in the back field, somehow what Mr. Goodwyn said didn't make a lot of sense.

"Okay, you know where to stand, Rachel?"

Unfortunately, I did. I took my place in front of the broken gate leading to the back field. The barn door the cattle were supposed to aim for was over to my left. I watched Michael pull in next to the barn and hitch a wagon to the tractor. He walked over, gave me a thumbs-up and leaned against the fence.

Great, now I couldn't back down.

Mr. Goodwyn marched in big rubber boots across the barnyard.

"Okay, Anna," he shouted through cupped hands. "You get Boomerang started and I'll get the rest to follow."

Anna seemed to know exactly what to do. She singled out Boomerang, slapped him on the rear and yelled, "Yaw!"

Yaw? But it worked. Because Boomerang sprang forward, lumbering in the direction of the barn. Or the back field. At that point it was hard to tell. Wherever he was going, it was quite quickly, and with Mr. Goodwyn's help he soon had nineteen cattle following his lead. I stood in front of the gate, rocking from foot to foot.

"Boomerang," I whispered. "To your right. Choose the barn door. To your right, boy."

Boomerang mooed loudly as Anna ran behind him.

"Yaw, yaw," she continued yelling.

"Anna! Never mind with the yaw, he's coming fast enough!"

"Don't worry. Remember, they're afraid of you," Mr. Goodwyn shouted.

I looked at the brown-and-white mass hurtling toward me. I didn't want to be rude and disagree with Mr. Goodwyn, but they couldn't have been half as frightened of me as I was of them.

"Please, Boomerang!" I began popping up and down. He was coming right at me. What if I didn't look scary? What if this was the day he broke with tradition? What if I arrived home in an envelope, a paper-thin scarecrow, trampled by cows?

"Anna!"

"Don't move just yet!"

I didn't *care* anymore that Michael was watching! I got ready to leap into the pile of manure next to me. But I didn't have to, because ten feet in front of me Boomerang swung to my left. All nineteen cattle followed him through the barn door.

Mr. Goodwyn plodded back across the barnyard in his rubber boots to where I stood with my knees knocking. He ruffled my hair.

"Rachel, you did real good, kid. We'll make you into a farm hand yet."

I didn't think that was very likely. Not if I ever had to do that again.

By the time I had picked my way back along the fence and met up with Anna and Michael, Mrs. Goodwyn had emerged from the barn. She had good news — thanks to Uncle Colin the injured deer was going to make it. And in a small gesture of triumph, she wiped her hands across her apron, told us that lunch would be in an hour and crossed the road into the house. We walked together around to the side of the barn. Michael swung up onto the tractor.

"I'm driving over to fix the fence in the back field. You guys want to come along?"

"I can't," Anna nodded in the direction of the

garden. "I promised Mom I'd pick some rhubarb. Take Rachel. I'll meet you guys back at the house in an hour."

There was nowhere for me to sit, so I stood, balancing on the trailer hitch and holding onto the back of the tractor seat. We bumped slowly up a hill, through an open gate and into the back field. Michael drove the tractor along the line of the fence until we began to go downhill where the dirt tracks curved through a small wood. We followed them next to the creek. It was cool in there, chugging beneath the shade of the old poplar trees, watching the leaves play tricks with the bits of light that filtered through. We crossed the creek by driving over a concrete sluiceway and continued up through the woods on the other side.

As we drove, we didn't talk much; the engine was too loud. But it was fun just standing up there behind Michael. His eyes were so quick, he'd point out a gopher or a hawk or a single wild lily nearly lost in the grass by the riverbank. Once we even saw a swift fox running through the woods, but except for that I missed most everything else so that I had to ask him what he'd seen. We crossed one more field after we were out of the woods.

The wind had blown two posts down, but they were not rotten, which Michael checked for first. I held them straight while he packed gravel and earth around the base. Then we stamped it level with the rest of the ground. Michael tightened the barbed wire and hammered the staples into place. I watched, helping when

I could, but mostly just standing there, amazed at how easily he took control of the barbed wire and tugged it all together.

"Where did you learn how to do all this stuff?" I finally asked.

He shrugged. "I've picked it up here and there."

"No, really. It's impressive."

"Think so?" He stopped what he was doing and leaned back against a post.

"Yeah, I think so. Not many guys can wield a hammer the way you do. At least, not the ones that I know. I've been watching and you've hit every staple on the first whack, like you've been doing it all your life."

He grinned. "I have been doing it all my life." Michael pounded another staple in the fence, and then, hesitating a little like he wasn't too sure he wanted to tell me, but he didn't want to hold out on me either, he said, "I guess I learned it from my brother, Nick."

"Oh." I handed him another staple and sat back on the edge of the trailer. It occurred to me, "Michael, didn't you tell me that you don't have any brothers or sisters?"

"Yeah, I did tell you that. And I don't. Not anymore. Nick was killed two years ago. He ran into a transport truck on the highway after his grad party. He died instantly, along with his girlfriend." He pounded the last staple into place.

I was almost thankful for the small, intrusive sound. Although, when it stopped, "God, Michael, I'm so sorry," was still all I could think of to say.

It sounded so inadequate. To be honest, I had very little experience with death. Our dog, Beatrice had died the year before, and nothing had ever hurt so much that I could remember. I couldn't even imagine if it had been Sean. But with Beatrice, it did get better, and after a while I was sad when I thought about her but I got used to her not being there. I don't know, it's such a feeble excuse and I've gone over it a hundred times in my head, but I can't think of any other reason why I didn't dig deeper at the time. Why I accepted it so easily when Michael answered, "It was tough for awhile. But now it's okay." That, and the fact that Michael could be so convincing.

He began to gather up the tools. "That's it. We're done."

When I didn't reply, he tapped me gently on a knee with the hammer. My leg jumped a bit. He laughed.

"Good, she's still got life in her. Come on, Rachel. Are you going to make me load all this stuff by myself?"

I helped him load the tools in the trailer. When we were done, Michael jumped on the tractor seat and turned the key in the ignition. The engine coughed and roared.

"Come on up," he shouted, "you're going to drive."

"But I don't know how."

"Don't worry," Michael moved back on the seat, leaving a small space in front of him for me to slide into. "You won't be driving alone."

I climbed up and sat down.

"Okay," he said, adjusting his body so that we fit together. It was a perfect fit and I settled back against him, which, I think surprised him because he went silent for a moment. His next word got caught in my hair. "Okay," he said a second time. Bringing his arms up, over my shoulders, he took hold of the gearshift. "Grab on to the steering wheel and steer."

Michael released the brake, pushed in the clutch and pulled back on the gearshift. Huh! I imagined us leaving the General Lee in a cloud of dust as I grabbed onto the steering wheel and we chugged across the field.

THREE

I only got scared twice during *Nightmare on Elm Street*. The first time was when Nancy woke up from a nightmare holding Freddy's hat. The second time was when the detectives were leaving the room where Glen was killed. Not that they showed the body or anything, but I don't usually get frightened at the obvious stuff anyway — the supposed-to-be-dead-springing-to-life scenes, the blood being sprayed across the walls. Those kinds of gimmicks make you jump or they gross you out, but they're almost always predictable. It's the psychological stuff that really gets to me. Come to think of it, there was a lot of that in *Nightmare on Elm Street*. No wonder my knees went weak when I tried to stand.

"That's good," Michael told me, taking my hand as we left the Roxy Theatre. "That means you're a sophisticated horror fan. Blood and bodies are for simpletons.

Take it from me, the scariest parts are always up here."
He tapped the side of his head.

"Michael, I don't want to disappoint you, but just
because you talked me into going to one horror movie
does *not* make me a fan."

He laughed. Michael carried a Super Soaker 3000.
The water gun had been a door prize won by me, but
given to him. Every Monday afternoon during the summer, the Roxy Theatre showed old movies to raise
money for the Downtown Preservation Society, and
anyone who donated five dollars was eligible for the
draw.

As we walked along Broadway toward the clinic
where I was meeting Anna, Michael spun the gun around
and around.

"Man, sometimes I wish I was a kid again. The toys
they have now are so cool. All I had was a Super Soaker
50. But with this —" he pumped it, "I could hit Taylor
right between the eyes from thirty yards away."

We had crossed the street and were passing Mac-
Pherson's Drug Store when Michael suddenly stopped,
backed up and peered in the window of the store.

"Wait here. I'll be right back."

"What is it?"

He only flicked me a mysterious smile as he opened
the door. A bell jangled and the door closed behind
him. Now *I* peered through the window, watching
Michael as he slowly sauntered down an aisle. Stop-
ping to leaf through a magazine, he shifted the water

gun onto his shoulder. He was in full view of a boy of about seven, who I guessed was somehow related to Mr. MacPherson because he sat behind the counter breaking open rolls of new coins. His eyes were fastened on the Super Soaker. After a minute, Michael returned the magazine to its stand and continued to cruise down the aisle. He reached the back counter, grinned widely and offered the boy the water gun. I laughed because the little guy was so amazed he just sat there, staring at it, like he was afraid to touch it in case it followed Michael back out the door.

"That was so *nice!*" I told Michael when he was back.

"Bradley's a great kid. I've already promised him he can take over the cave when I get out of this place in a couple of years."

We had reached the clinic.

"And where are you going?"

"That —" Michael smiled and tapped the side of his head, "is all up here."

"Ahh, right," I nodded. "With all the scary stuff."

He laughed. "I'll meet you at Dot's later?"

Michael had to help Scott and his dad move patio blocks, so we arranged to meet at Dot's Diner at four.

■ ■ ■

An hour later, Anna and I sat in a red vinyl booth in Dot's Diner, eating pizza, waiting for Michael and Scott.

Cory and Taylor and their friend, Simon Ferguson, were sprawled in a booth across the aisle. Simon was laughing at Taylor, who was loosening the lid on the salt so that the next person who shook it would get the entire bottle on their plate. Remarkably juvenile, Anna had already informed him. Cory was sipping a Slurpee and flicking a lighter on and off.

I was looking out the window at the black car parked in front of Dot's Diner. It was rusted a little around the back wheels and it was amazingly long. It was so long, I had to strain my neck to see where it began and where it ended.

"Lovely, isn't it?" Anna bit into her pizza.

Velvet curtains hung along the side and back windows.

Anna jerked a thumb toward the table across from us. "That's Taylor's very own limousine. Can you believe it? Two tons of steel and that much attitude? It's a disaster waiting to happen. His dad gave it to him last month when he turned sixteen. He bought a new one for the funeral home."

I squinted. A small skull dangled from the rearview mirror and a silver serpent had been painted on the hood.

Anna screwed up her face. "He customized it."

We both looked over at Taylor.

"Beauty, eh?"

I was about to tell him, no, it was not beautiful, it was just about the tackiest thing I'd ever seen, but I was stopped by the look on his face. Why destroy him? He obviously loved that limousine.

"Yeah, beauty," I said. I turned back to my pizza.

Dot was leaning over the front counter reading *The Agatha Bulletin*. She was quite an old lady and she didn't always hear that well. Because of this, I had discovered that you didn't always get what you ordered — but she was so nice it would have been mean to complain.

Although that day I was tempted. I had specifically ordered pizza *without* anchovies because there is nothing more disgusting. They look, smell, and taste disgusting, and now — here was practically a whole school of them swimming beneath the cheese! Anna sighed, snatched the plate away from me and began picking them off with a fork.

I glanced up at Dot who was dabbing tears from her eyes as she read the front-page story. I happened to know the story she was reading was about Mr. Baker being gored by Shainberg's bull. He had been a sick old man and while his son was rounding up cattle he had become confused and taken a wrong turn into the neighbor's bull paddock. Uncle Colin had explained that it was one of those very tragic things that can happen on a farm.

Next to us, Cory and his friends were becoming very loud, trying to impress us. Simon was talking about how he'd pressed 180 pounds in the gym that morning. On Saturday, Cory reached 160 kilometers an hour on his brother's Harley. Simon's dad was buying a home movie theater with surround sound.

I saw Taylor glance in the direction of Dot at the counter. "Oh, yeah?" He picked a french fry from his plate, leaned back and threw an arm across the back of the bench seat. He munched on the french fry as he spoke. "Well beat this. We've got old man Baker chilling in our basement."

Huh? Anna and I looked over at their table.

Taylor picked up his knife. "It went all the way through," he told us. "From the front to the back." By moving the knife alongside his head, he demonstrated the horn's path through Mr. Baker. Our eyes stayed glued to the knife. It stopped. "My dad found the eyeball stuck right back here in the hollow of his neck."

Ick. I shivered.

"He would know," Anna whispered. "His dad owns the funeral home. They live upstairs."

"Want to see him?"

We looked over at Taylor.

"Bet you've never seen a dead guy before."

What he said was true. I never had seen a dead person. Except for fake ones in the movies.

"At least, not with a horn stuck through his head."

That was even more true, and for one very small second Taylor had me curious, but the whole thing was way too gruesome and the notion quickly passed. Just then the door opened and Scott and Michael stepped inside. Scott lifted a hand, strolled over to our booth and slid next to Anna. Michael sat down on the bench next to me. Anna pushed the pizza in front of them. Michael didn't want any, but Scott said he was starved.

"Hey, Cardinal?"

Raising the pizza to his mouth, Scott looked over at Cory, who was watching him.

"Coming with us?"

Scott bit off a big chunk and chewed hungrily. "Where?"

"We're going to check out old man Baker. He's in cold storage in Sparshatt's basement."

Michael, who was picking dog hair off my shirt, glanced over at Cory. "Sparks, that Slurpee has gone to your head. I think you ought to slow down."

But Scott ordered a Coke before answering. "Now what would I want to see old man Baker for?"

Taylor jumped right in. "Because they're coming with us." He thrust a finger in our direction.

Anna and I gaped at him.

Cory stood up. Simon and Taylor followed his cue. "Let's go."

Michael and Scott looked to us for an answer. We both opened our eyes wide and shook our heads fiercely.

"Forget it." Scott took another bite of pizza.

"Why not?"

"Because I'm eating my lunch."

Cory tilted his chin in the air. He looked at each of our faces before flashing a shrewd, white grin.

"It's because you're chicken," he decided, resting his eyes on Scott.

Taylor, munching on another french fry, laughed. "Cardinal's afraid to look at a dead guy!"

All three of them laughed.

I felt Michael's hand stiffen on my arm. And after what had happened in the cave, and after what Anna said he would do in a second, I almost expected him to squash the french fry in Taylor's face. But he managed to stay right where he was. He only said, "Maybe if we ignore them they'll go away."

We did manage to ignore them. For a while. Until Taylor refused to drop it.

"What's the matter, Cardinal? Do dead guys give you the creeps?"

"Yeah," echoed Simon. "One glimpse of a stiff and you can't sleep at night?"

I knew they were just being idiots. I mean, I knew they were not deliberately trying to taunt Michael. Still, it was a cruel thing to say.

Unable to ignore them any longer, Michael jumped to his feet, jerked the salt from Taylor's hand and flipped it, dumping the whole bottle over his plate.

"Hey! Jerk!" Taylor snatched hold of his arm. "What'd you do that for?"

Michael answered by gripping Taylor's arm, twisting it back and pinning it against the back of the bench seat. At the same time he drove an elbow into his neck. Taylor immediately swung his free fist up to club him, but Cory reached across the table and intervened. Holding Taylor by the wrist, he nodded toward the front counter where Dot had looked up from the paper.

Taylor glanced in her direction, then glowered at Michael. "Asshole," he growled. Reluctantly, he dropped his arm.

Michael walked out the door.

"Michael," I started to go after him, but Scott gave me a sign that I should just let him go. He turned and glared at Cory.

"All right." Flinging the pizza on the plate in front of him, he stood up. "I'll look at your dead guy. Come on. We'll all look at your dead guy. We'd love to see him, wouldn't we, girls?"

Anna and I stared at each other in horror. Scott nudged us to our feet and while I paid Dot, Anna brushed the mess of salt onto a plate and dumped it in the trash. Scott plowed past Cory.

"All right, lead the way, Taylor. Let's go see this dead guy with a hole through his head."

And before Anna and I knew it, we were sitting in Taylor's long limousine. I was in the front seat, between Cory and Taylor, who kept flicking salt from his lap. Anna, Simon and Scott were a long way behind. Taylor pulled the key from the visor over his head, stuck it in the ignition and started the car. We drove down Broadway with the grisly little skull pitching back and forth.

"You're sure no one's home?" Simon asked Taylor.

"Nobody's home. They've gone to my grandmother's. They won't be home until late."

Once we had turned off Broadway, Taylor drove like an idiot. He sped down the straight stretches and careened around corners. He laughed with Cory when I was thrown between their laps.

"Taylor, you moron!" shrieked Anna, struggling to get the words out.

Taylor veered around another corner and Simon yelped as he hit his head. Scott moved forward, fighting to maintain his balance. His hands clamped hard onto Taylor's shoulders.

"Slow down, Sparshatt, or your dad's going to be pickling all of us tonight!"

Taylor did slow down. He came to a stop next to a small sign. We were parked in front of Sparshatt's Funeral Home, a brick two-storey on a shady street. Cory and Taylor stepped out of the car. I didn't want to, but Taylor reached in and grabbed me by the arm.

The houses were old and large and they looked expensive. Most of them had concrete porches and broad maple trees reaching forty feet into the sky. Taylor's house was the only one with an awning, a quiet tunnel leading from the sidewalk to the front door. We walked beneath it, then around the side of the house to a door at the back.

Taylor unlocked the door while we waited. Anna and I stood behind Cory and Scott, then followed them onto a landing with Simon herding us in from behind.

To our right, a half flight of stairs covered in a rich burgundy carpet led up. To our left, concrete steps led down. It was still and quiet and it felt eery being there. It also felt very, very wrong. I looked at Anna. We began to back up, but Simon stood squarely behind us, blocking the door. Taylor flicked on a light in the basement and solemnly, we walked down.

The floor was shiny white linoleum and there was a hospital odor of strong disinfectant, which seemed to be masking some other harsh chemical smell. Three doors led off the hall from where we stood at the bottom of the stairs. Two were wide open. One led to a utility area with a furnace, taps and a large washbasin. Another to a storage room with bicycles and boots and fishing rods propped against the wall. The third door was locked. There was only a deadbolt, no doorknob or other way to open it.

"Move!" ordered Taylor, pulling Simon from the bottom step. Taylor lifted the last tread, which was on a hinge, like the lid of a box. He took out a key and passed it before our eyes.

"He still has no idea I know about this," he gloated. He unlocked the door.

Cory hissed at Anna and me. "You girls ready for this?"

We moved closer to Scott. Taylor reached an arm inside the door and flipped on the light switch. Light glanced off the countertops; it bounced from the shiny stark floor. It sprang full in our faces. It was a light far brighter than in any normal room.

Once we were used to it, I tried to bring myself to look inside. Remaining in the hall, I stole just the tiniest peek around the doorway. I looked away. I had seen only glaring walls and a pair of thin, gray feet. Mr. Baker lay on a table about ten feet away, and only a wall stood between me and the rest of his very dead body. It gave me a sick, dizzy feeling and I leaned against the doorjamb. This was a terrible — and a very real — thing that had happened to Mr. Baker, which I now had little doubt was the point Scott was intending to make to Cory and Taylor when he agreed to come along.

"Well, ladies, after you," Taylor invited with annoying politeness.

Scott stepped in front of us. "No. We'll follow you in. After all, it is your house."

Taylor hesitated before taking a deep breath. Signaling Simon to follow, he walked boldly into the bright white room. Simon marched in after him.

"Wimps," he quipped as he passed by us.

Cory did not follow but also leaned against the wall. Scott held an arm before Anna and me like this was a controlled crossing. Like he needed to protect us from walking in to marvel at Mr. Baker. As if we had any intention of doing that.

He held up his other hand. And he listened. He listened and he waited for a reaction from Simon and Taylor. When they were well into the room, he let his arm drop. He eyed Cory, who was staring at the floor.

"What's wrong, Sparks? Not up for a little blood and guts?"

Cory looked at him, then we all looked at Simon and Taylor who came staggering back with their faces blank. Taylor's puffed chest had collapsed and he held one hand to his trembling mouth. The other was clamped to his stomach. Simon ran to the utility room and threw up in the washbasin. They both sank on their knees to the floor.

They were still on their knees, their faces as pale as peeled potatoes, when the door to the landing suddenly opened. A deep voice called, "Taylor? Taylor! Is that you down there?"

Taylor's father! Grasping our hands, Scott pulled us down the hall and through the utility room. Cory was close at our heels. They both knew about a door leading from the basement outside to the back yard. Scott flung it open and we pounded up the concrete steps. We bolted across the Sparshatts' back yard and turned up the alley. We stopped behind a garage to catch our breath. Through the open door we could hear Mr. Sparshatt's angry voice, shattering the silence of the funeral home.

FOUR

It was hot. Hotter than anything I'd known, and I was melting. Anna and I had stopped by the cave to cool off. We were going swimming at Palliser Point Park where the rattlesnakes nest. I was not exactly thrilled by the idea, but Anna assured me, "It's the best place to swim in town. Besides, they won't do anything unless you disturb them." She sat across from me, fanning herself with her hand. "Or step on them."

Let's just say I was glad that she was going to be leading the way.

"All right, Rachel." Anna stood up. "Let's go. I'm going to turn into a lump of wax if I sit here any longer."

From the top of the bluff, we picked our way down a steep path into Buffalo Coulee. Once on flat ground, the path ran next to the river for half a mile. We took great swigs from our water bottles and squirted them over our heads and sometimes at each other. More than once I scratched my bare legs on the stubby wolf willows, which separated the river from the path.

As I walked behind Anna, I thought about Michael and Taylor and what had happened in Dot's Diner. I thought about Michael and Cory in the cave. I brushed a willow branch aside.

"Anna, do you think those guys are serious? Do you think they'd ever get carried away?"

"You mean Scott and Cory and those guys?" Anna slapped a mosquito from her arm. "Naw, it's harmless. They've been like that since I can remember. It's just some kind of power thing. A guy thing, I suppose."

I wasn't so sure and I told her that. "They seemed pretty serious to me. Particularly Michael."

Anna lifted her hair from her neck, shook it and sighed. "Yeah, well, that's not because of Cory and Taylor. Michael just gets caught up in his own problems sometimes. Hey, what'd you think of *Something About Mary*?"

I was about to say, huh? but I quickly remembered that *Something About Mary* was the movie I was supposed to have watched at Michael's house the night before. And actually we did play it. We just didn't watch it. Much.

"It was good," I said, not very convincingly.

"What do you mean good? It was hilarious." She turned and frowned, then, clueing in, she smiled a little. "You guys didn't even watch it, did you?"

I felt my face flush. "Parts."

She laughed. "The parts when you came up for air."

We jumped an uprooted stump and followed a curve in the path.

"Anna, what do you mean Michael gets caught up in his own problems?"

"Oh nothing, really. Sometimes he just pulls inside. He shuts us out. But it's not really the way Michael is. He's still dealing with Nick's accident, and anyway, it usually doesn't last that long. Look. Here we are. Palliser Point Park."

Coming up next to Anna, I looked around. She couldn't possibly mean the flat, dry wasteland that stretched before us.

"This is it?" And I could not even try to pretend to hide my disappointment because this was nothing like the parks I knew. I was expecting something cool and green. Here, there was no grass at all. It was like some weird, whimsical world created by Dr. Seuss. The ground was nothing but hot gray mud that limped forward in waves baked by the sun. It was broken only by a few stunted cottonwoods sprouting twisted black limbs.

"Come on, Rachel."

I followed Anna as she led the way through a heavy thicket of willows down to the river, all the time thinking that I would not be surprised if we ran into the Pale Green Pants along the way.

We had worn our bathing suits beneath our T-shirts and shorts, and after peeling hers off, Anna waded into the water. I stood ankle deep in the sludge on the bank. A horsefly circled my head.

"Anna, I can't swim in this."

Anna, who was already waist deep in the river, slipped in and rolled to float on her back. I looked nervously at the ground around my feet. No thin slippery heads poised to sink their fangs into me. I bent down and listened to the grass. No soft rattling sounds on the shore.

"Let's go!"

I jumped as Anna's big voice came volleying across the water. She pointed to a heavy black cloud that hadn't existed five minutes earlier. I shrugged. The thunderhead appeared to be a long way off, but Anna was clawing her way back to the muddy bank already.

"What's the panic?" I asked as she changed into her shorts. "It's got to be miles from here."

"Yeah, miles and about five minutes. Come on, Rachel, pick up that stuff."

I picked up the bag and towels as she asked, and in the short time it took me to do it, the sun that hadn't blinked since I arrived in Agatha was gone. We fought our way back through the willows as the first raindrops began to fall.

The cracked mud surface quickly became slick, then slimy. We skidded across it, headed for the path we had to follow to climb back up the cliff. We began to jog. Lightning flashed across the distant sky. There was a horrendous crash, like something not far from us had been struck. Thunder followed, a heart-stopping force roaring down on us. We started to run. The rain beat our bare skin and within minutes churned the dry waves of road mud into a thick glutinous sea. We fought gravity to wade through it, but it became harder and harder as the gumbo — it actually had a name! — strapped itself in layers around our feet. Finally we made it to the path.

Running became easier on the hard-packed surface, but the rain hit our faces like bits of metal. It poured down in a violent mass. Our clothes were soaked and I blinked furiously in an attempt to get rid of the rain that clouded my eyes. The water roared past in the river next to us. It carried leaves, garbage, a small tree and a cow! A dead cow.

"Anna, look!"

The big bloated thing turned in the water with its stiff legs straight up. It stalled for a moment on a clump of grass, but the current was swift and it pushed and pulled and dislodged the cow, spun it twice and carried it away.

"Never mind. Come on."

We continued to push our way through the long musty grass. We stumbled up the path from Buffalo Coulee to the top of the bluff, keeping our heads bent, terrified of being struck by lightning. Finally, floundering like newly hatched geese, we tumbled into the cave.

We were surprised to find Michael and Scott inside. They had also been caught in the storm and had cut up the bluff from the highway, where they'd left their bikes at the end of the path. They were adjusting the position of the cattle trough, dragging it further from the wall to catch the run-off now spilling through the skylight. When they were done, Scott marched across the ground, with the sound of water squashing from his running shoes, and dropped into a chair.

Hauling a soggy towel from my bag, I attempted to dry my face and sopping hair. While I was doing it, Michael came up behind me and pulled me to him. His skin was wet, but it was warm and there was something so simple and nice about being all wet and close like that. I folded my arms across his, and together we watched the rain continue to hurtle down from where we stood in the mouth of the cave.

It wasn't very long before Michael was pointing to the west where the sky was blue and bright again, and as quickly as the rain had come, it stopped. The sun came out and the heat was on our faces. We turned back into the cave.

"I bet someone just lost a few cattle." Scott still sat in the chair, where he chewed a long piece of prairie grass. "Or a roof. Or their barn."

Anna was perched on the arm of the chair with her legs across Scott's lap, pulling her fingers through his damp hair. Behind them, water trickled through the skylight and splashed into the cattle trough.

"That kind of storm usually means a tornado," she explained to me. "Probably a small one touched down on a ranch somewhere." Something outside caught her attention. Looking past me, her eyes suddenly grew large. "Rib Bone!" she squealed, jumping off the chair.

We all turned toward the river to see Rib Bone, his white hair flowing, supporting himself on a stick, hobbling off the train trestle. He continued down the railroad tracks toward town.

Scott followed Anna to where she peeked from behind a wall, staring after Rib Bone. He stood in the entrance to the cave.

"Mike, come here. Check out the size of the hunting knife sticking out of Rib Bone's back pocket."

Michael moved next to him. He whistled through his teeth. "Big enough to carve the heart out of a bull moose with one twist. Or Anna if she got in his way."

I squinted hard to see this big hunting knife, but I saw nothing. By that time, Scott and Michael were laughing hard.

"Oh sure, you guys think it's a big joke." Anna shrank further into the shadow of the cave. "But what kind of person needs a knife like that?"

"Anna, it was a joke. There *is* no knife," I told her.

"Hey," Michael suddenly punched Scott on the arm. "Let's go check out Rib Bone's Chevy. I want to see if he's got the engine rebuilt yet."

"Michael, are you nuts?" Anna exploded. "That's trespassing. Even if he is a murderer."

"Come on, Anna. Scott and I have been over there dozens of times. Rib Bone wouldn't care. He's refinishing this cool '55 Chevy he bought three years ago. I just want to see how it's progressed. Come on, Rachel." And I guess, expecting me to follow him, Michael left the cave.

Scott shrugged. "We should probably go with him."

Shielding her eyes, gazing down the railroad tracks in the direction that Rib Bone had gone, Anna looked after Michael, who was already well on his way across the bluff. "Michael!"

Michael didn't respond.

"Oooh, I suppose you're right. Okay, let's go."

We had to move fast to catch up with Michael. We jogged up next to him, then along the railroad tracks and down to the train trestle where everyone trotted on. Except me. The thing is, I don't like heights. I peered between the ties. It was a long, long way down to the river.

"Come on, Rachel." Anna waved for me to follow her.

"But there are spaces between the tracks."

"Yeah?"

"Well, I can see through them."

"Yes, and so can I. But if you put one foot in front of the other and you don't look down, you'll be absolutely fine."

Maybe. But I wasn't so sure.

"How do you know there isn't a train coming?"

"We already saw one go by. There won't be another one for hours."

"Come on, Rach, don't be a city wuss," said Michael. And I guess to prove that a train trestle was no more dangerous than monkey bars, in a matter of seconds Michael had shimmied ten feet up a cross beam. Anchoring himself by his feet and holding on with only one arm, he swung out high above the river.

Anna screamed and my stomach dropped to my toes.

Michael jumped back to the track again. "See — a piece of cake."

"Michael! Are you crazy? What if you fell?!" shrieked Anna.

"Well, I didn't. So, there's nothing to worry about." Michael grinned and spread his arms wide. Pulling an arm around me, he steered me onto the train trestle. "Come on. It's easy. We just step from tie to tie."

So I did. Although my legs wobbled and I was almost on my knees by the time we got to the other side. We crept up the stubbly hill through goldenrod and horsetails to the back of Rib Bone's cabin, which was just on the other side of the ridge. The cabin was Rasmussen's old homestead and it was small, weathered and gray. Most of the homesteads I'd seen dotting the prairies were crumbling into the ground. The winter winds swept through them and they leaned heavily in one direction.

Rib Bone's cabin was ancient, but it stood straight, with real windows and doors that closed. A few feet to the east was a large shed with a graying woodpile leaning against one wall. The yard was not so much messy, but a busy place, with tools lying scattered around, dropped where they'd been used. A thriving vegetable garden sprawled in the sun, looking strangely out of place in the midst of all the sand and dust. We walked around to the front of the cabin, where Anna and I crouched behind a large boulder left when glaciers moved across the prairies millions of years ago. Michael opened the door of the shed and Scott followed him inside.

"What do you think?" Anna shrugged. "I mean, since we're here. I guess it wouldn't hurt to take one little peek in his cabin, just through the window. It's not like we'd be touching his stuff or anything like that."

"Oh, I don't know, Anna."

"Come on, Rachel. I just want to see inside." Anna left the rock and crept across the yard. All alone, I glanced over my shoulder, knowing that when Rib Bone returned, I'd be the first one he'd stumble on.

"Anna, wait." I caught up to her. We crept to the window, cupped our hands to our faces and, standing on tiptoes, squinted inside the cabin. It was one big room and there was very little furniture. What furniture there was, was rough, and I guessed that Rib Bone had made it himself. Directly in front of us was a heavy wooden table with an open book on it. An iron bed stood in one corner, and next to it was a set of bookshelves and a cabinet with glass doors. A few menacing-looking tools and a shotgun were stored inside it. A woodburning stove sat in the center of the room. That was about it. There was no telephone, no stereo, no microwave, no computer and there was no TV.

"He doesn't have very much stuff," Anna whispered.

Scott, who had left the shed and come up behind us, overheard her. "How much stuff does one old hermit need?"

He made a good point. Uncle Colin had told me that Rib Bone had been a prospector most of his life. He'd spent a lot of time alone in the mountains and woods, searching for gold.

"Which," he'd said, "is the reason he prefers to live the way he does. He's comfortable living on his own."

Anna continued to insist it was because he was completely weird.

The sound of the shed door closing made me jump. Michael came up next to me and looked in the window. We both caught a flash of movement near the stove.

"Hey, it's Watson." Michael didn't even lower his voice when he said it. "Man, he's still alive!"

We all stared at the golden retriever, who was still curled up, but with much effort had lifted his head from the floor. His muzzle was as white and as grizzled as the hair on old Rib Bone's head. He blinked in the sun, stretched his nose ever so slightly and struggled up on his feet. He choked on a bark.

"I forgot about Watson." Scott squinted. "He didn't even hear us until now. The old boy's blind and he's as deaf as a stone."

The dog took a step forward and stumbled. Standing where he was, he tried hard to sniff in what he could.

"Come on," said Scott, "we should get out of here.

We didn't come over here to kill Rib Bone's dog by giving him a heart attack."

Anna and I agreed with him, not wanting to give Rib Bone *any* reason to come after us. Other than his natural urge to murder. So after hiking back down the hill, we crossed the train trestle and followed the river out to the highway where Scott and Michael had left their bikes.

"How's Rib Bone's Chevy coming along?" I pointed to a large knot of roots bulging from the path.

Michael jumped it. "I don't know. It's a lot of work for an old guy like that. He's still got a long way to go."

FIVE

"Look at that!" Michael used his paddle to point to the bird gliding over our heads. "A bald eagle. Man, its wingspan must be six feet across."

The river carried us beneath the train trestle. Once on the other side, we watched the eagle bank and turn.

"He sees something."

Michael was right. A hundred feet ahead of us the bird plunged into the water. Seconds later it was climbing high again with a fish twisting from one of its great claws. Raising a hand to block the sun from his eyes, Michael squinted after the eagle.

"It's a pike," he told us. He pulled the paddle through the muddy water again. "Rachel, don't slice the water, pull the paddle flat against it."

"I'm trying. It just keeps getting away."

We were canoeing down the river from Rotary Park to Armstrong's Stables, a half-day trip. Mr. Armstrong had loaned us his two canoes, and despite my clumsy paddling, Michael and I were three canoe lengths ahead of Scott and Anna and Sylvie Hagen, Anna's friend. Sylvie had been camping in Jasper with her parents for the past two weeks. Scott was steering, Anna was in the bow wearing a red visor, and Sylvie was sprawled in the middle, suntanning, like she was some kind of Egyptian queen.

The river was calm and smooth and it was easy to maneuver. Except for the hollow echo of my paddle against the canoe, we slid along its brown surface almost without sound. The sandy bank stretched fifteen feet back to the base of the bluffs, which rose high above us all along the river. In some places, like Buffalo Coulee, they rose as a staircase of rumpled hills, bald and rippled with deep ridges. Through these dry creek beds, animal paths wound down to the river from the flat plain above. In other places along the river, we faced nothing but sheer white walls.

To my left, the mouth of the cave looked like a smudge on the sandstone, a spot missed by the sun. To my right, I could see the small white plume of smoke from Rib Bone's stove drift off into the sky.

I pulled my paddle through the water. There was a sandbar ahead of us. Michael had already seen it. He steered us around it, through the narrower channel of deep water. Scott followed his lead.

We were animal-watching. Michael had already pointed out the bald eagle and, earlier, a pelican soaring in a wide circle above the river. He was the first to spot two mule deer that had come down to the river to drink. Sylvie heard a coyote. Not far away from us, we could hear its sad, pitiful howl and, not long after, the yapping as it was answered by a crowd.

But I still pride myself. I was the one who spied the white-tailed deer. I almost fell out of the canoe, shaking my arm, trying to get everyone to look at the mother bounding along the ridge at the top of the bluff. She was followed closely by her fawn, who worked hard, bouncing behind her like a bright-eyed little puppet on springs.

It was amazingly hot and still. Sylvie poured more suntan lotion on Anna's shoulders when she noticed they were turning pink. Michael peeled off his shirt. Scott filled an empty jug with river water, leaned back and let it slowly trickle over his head.

For a while, we tied our canoes together, tucked our paddles along the sides, cracked open Cokes, kicked back and just drifted. I rolled up towels, which Michael and I propped beneath our heads, and together we lay in the stern and watched the few tufts of cloud wander by. I pulled close to him, and as he stroked my arm I realized how in just three weeks so much about him had become so familiar. He lifted a strap from my shoulder and kissed the spot where it had been.

"Michael," I said, "we're not alone."

A fact which obviously didn't bother him as much as it bothered me, because he said, "I don't care."

But he lifted the strap back onto my shoulder again.

Tracing small circles on his back, I felt how his skin drew the heat of the sun, and I wished I could have stayed like that — with the warmth of his body against mine, drifting with the current, listening to the rhythmic slap of the water against the canoe — all day.

"Sandbar alert!" The clunk of Anna's paddle against our canoe broke that rhythm. "Come on, Michael, we need you to steer."

He groaned a little.

"I guess you're needed," I told him.

Michael resisted.

"Come on, Michael." Anna hit the canoe again.

"All right, all right." Michael dropped his head off my shoulder. "But I'd rather stay here and run aground."

We sat up and Michael and Scott guided us past another sandbar. Once the crisis was past, Michael dove off the stern of the canoe into the river. He turned and swam along next to me with quiet strokes and the sun glinting off his curly black hair.

"Did Scott ever tell you about the time he pulled a dead guy from the river?" He was back in the canoe, shaking water from his ears.

"Uh, no," I said. "It's never come up." I threw him a towel.

Anna sat up and finished her Coke. "She doesn't want to hear about it."

"Sure she does. You do, don't you, Rachel? Tell her Scott."

Scott was lying against the back of the canoe with

his eyes closed and his arms folded behind his head. He turned and looked at Michael. Noticing that we had drifted off course, he picked up a paddle and lazily steered us to the middle of the river.

"No, I don't think she does." He leaned back in the sun and closed his eyes.

I looked from one to the other. "Okay. This is not fair. I hate not knowing things. You *have* to tell me."

"Okay," said Michael. "If you force me to." He pulled his T-shirt on and settled back into the canoe. "It was three years ago." Michael checked with Scott, who nodded. "We were standing on the train trestle after one of those sudden storms and there was all kinds of stuff floating down the river. Tires and branches and junk. We even saw a drowned owl. Then we saw this one clump of deadwood, moving slowly, turning in circles. It looked like just a heap of sticks, but there was something red in it and we couldn't figure out what it was. So we ran down to the river before it hit the trestle. There was an arm, in a red shirtsleeve, sticking straight up out of the heap above everything else."

"You don't have to listen to him," Sylvie told me.

I glanced at her, then back to Michael. "An arm? Is this a joke?" Sometimes I didn't know whether to believe Michael's stories or not.

"Nope. Anyway, Scott jumped right in and swam after it."

"Why?"

"Because he's a do-gooder."

Scott frowned with his eyes still closed.

"He swam out to the heap. It had got stuck against a piling, and he reached over and pulled at the sleeve."

I grimaced. "And?"

"And the whole rotten arm came off in his hand."

"Gross!"

"I told you, you didn't have to listen to him," Sylvie reminded me.

"Michael, why do you always have to tell us that kind of stuff?" Anna untied the knot holding our canoes together.

"I don't know, Anna. Maybe it's the only kind of stuff I have to tell."

Anna didn't answer.

"Anyway," Michael spoke to me again, "he dropped the arm and swam back to shore like he'd been shot out of a cannon."

I noticed Scott had sat up and was beginning to paddle with a purpose.

"Who was it?"

"Some guy that had fallen off a boat two weeks earlier, south of Lethbridge. Scott, where are you going?"

"To shore. I want to see if that buffalo skull is still under that overhang."

That was the end of Michael's story. It got choked out in the sounds of paddles against gunwales, turning water and Scott giving orders to Anna. The bows of our canoes slid up onto the pebbly beach. My bare toes sank into the cool mud as I stepped into a foot of water and helped Michael drag the canoe a safe distance onto shore.

The buffalo skull was still there at the bottom of a very high cliff. Scott had long ago covered it with willow branches so that no one else would see it and take it home. He liked to look at it where the animal had fallen. He wanted to watch it become part of the beach. It was gray and wooden looking, and Scott figured it was easily more than a hundred years old.

Sylvie followed a cattle path up the side of a hill for fifty feet or so. She wanted to see where the bobcat tracks led. Before following her, Anna and I stopped to study the tracks.

"That's no bobcat," Anna said to me. She hollered up to Sylvie, "These tracks belong to a cougar."

Scott stood next to us. "Uh-huh," he said. "That's a cougar all right."

Sylvie quickly retraced her steps and jumped down. We picked our way along the shore, looking for the medicine wheel Michael swore he'd seen somewhere on his last trip. I had stupidly left my sandals in the canoe and was mostly concentrating on trying to avoid the heaps of freshwater mussels which cut into my bare feet.

Michael came upon the antelope first. It was lying in a bush with its tan chest all bright and bloody. A magnificent animal, it had sailed with muscles straining across the hot prairie that very morning. It had come down to cool itself in the river less than an hour before. Michael figured this from the pooling of its blood and the warmth still rising from its thick hide. Wasted now. The sight was shocking, it was frightening. The body of that antelope was lying there with a bloody stump where the head should have been.

"Poachers," Michael and Scott agreed.

Anna, Sylvie and I just felt sick.

"They're close," Scott said. "Not far from here. It would have taken them some time to cut it up."

"Creeps!" Sylvie shrieked.

"Who are they?"

"Who knows? Rich guys," Scott told me. "They pay big money to be brought in here and bag themselves a trophy. By Christmastime they'll be swilling eggnog, bragging to their friends about the antelope they snagged, pointing to the head they have mounted on the wall."

There was nothing we could do. We walked back to the canoes and continued down the river, barely saying five words between us for the next half an hour. Those are the kinds of things that take time to settle into your head, but once they do, they take hold and they stay with you a very long time.

The cliffs on either side of us were not so steep as we passed further east along the river, and in places it would have been quite easy to make our way to the top. There was more bush and a few twisted willows. Scott told us we were about five miles upstream from Armstrong's Stables. I was glad to hear it because I'd seen more than enough for one day. Sylvie had finished two Cokes since our last stop and she couldn't last five more miles without a stop in the bush. We parked our canoes next to some rocks and sat down on them, waiting for Sylvie, watching the pigeons flock on the other side of the river.

"Get down!" Scott suddenly shouted.

Without knowing what was going on, we all dove behind the rocks. Except Michael.

"What is it?" we whispered.

"It's them."

Anna and I lifted our heads and cautiously peered across the river. We could see two figures moving up the side of the bluff along a ridge through the silver leaves. I watched closely. There were actually three of them; one was several feet in the lead, the other two lagged behind, hauling a heavy sack.

None of them were big men but they somehow looked as if they were. They were thickened by heavy hunting vests and made taller by the guns they had slung across their shoulders. They struggled with the packs and gear and sack they carried, tripping over rocks and roots.

Usually Michael moved faster than any of us, but all he had time to get out before we pounced on him was, "Hey! Pigs!" The three of us saw the guns, saw him standing there ready to fight and we flattened him. Scott grabbed his ankles, I threw myself across his back and Anna stuffed her towel into his face. "Shut up, Michael. They'll kill us."

The three men stopped and turned and scanned the river. Not seeing anything, they continued to haul their load up the cliff. We lay on Michael while he thrashed and squirmed until they were well over the hill and out of sight. When we finally rolled off him, everyone was breathing heavily.

Michael spat sand from his mouth. "You're just going to let them go?!"

"Look at us!" Anna shouted. "We've got our shirts and our shorts and a whole lot of nice ideas! They've got guns, Michael, and an illegal antelope's head. Some things are just bigger than we are."

"Michael," I said, "Anna's right."

"Come on," said Scott, pulling Michael to his feet. "We'll talk to Phil Armstrong. Maybe there's something he can do."

When we finally arrived at Armstrong's Stables, we were tired and sunburnt and discouraged.

"Well," said Mr. Armstrong, as he helped us pull the canoes up onto the grass, "you look like a cheery bunch. A little too much of a good thing?"

SIX

If I had to name the day we began losing Michael, I would say it was on July 25, Simon's birthday. Anna and Scott disagree with me; they say it had really started long before. They are probably right. I just hadn't been around long enough to know.

Simon had a party on his birthday. I was not sure why Scott, Michael, Anna and I were invited, but we were. I asked Anna about this when I dropped by her house before we met Scott.

"Simon's okay," she told me, brushing her hair in front of the mirror in the hall. "As long as you get him alone. But then, so is Cory. Even Taylor can go soft once in a while." She pulled her hair back in a clip. "Okay, I'm ready. Let's go."

Scott was waiting for us outside and we all walked to Michael's house, which was on the other side of the tracks. Michael was in a bad mood from the time he closed his front door. Something had happened between him and his parents, but he refused to tell me what it was.

"Okay, okay," I said after trying to get it out of him without any luck. "Try and forget about it and concentrate on having a good time."

Which, I guess, is what he decided to do.

Simon's parents were out of town and his older brother had stocked the fridge with beer. I'm not much of a drinker, and if there was ever any chance of me becoming one, my friend Leslie throwing up in my lap at a party put all that on hold. But I had one beer that night to join Michael. An hour after we arrived I had made my way through half the bottle. In the same time Michael had downed three. It surprised me because it seemed out of character for him. He drank one more while Anna, Sylvie and I baked the burritos Simon pulled out of the freezer, even though both Scott and I told him to slow down.

Michael didn't want anything to eat. After arguing with Cory over the music he was choosing, Michael sat with me in a big chair in the living room. His hands were beginning to travel all over me, and even though everyone else was absorbed in who they were with or what they were doing, it was becoming embarrassing. I locked his fingers in mine. He wanted me to go with him into one of the bedrooms. He was pretty worked up, so I was hesitant.

"Come on, Rach. You told me to have a good time."

I thought about it. Maybe if we were alone I could

get him to talk. Maybe he would tell me what was wrong and why he was acting this way.

"If I do, will you tell me what's bugging you?"

"Yeah, yeah, whatever."

"All right," I agreed.

I took his hand and we threaded past people leaning in the doorways and sprawled across the hallway. The word had got out and Simon's friends had invited their friends to the party. Michael led me to a spare bedroom in the basement of the house.

"Okay," I said, sitting on the bed next to him, "what is it? What's going on?"

I don't like the taste of beer at the best of times and I sure didn't like getting it secondhand when he kissed me right then.

"Nothing's going on," he said, pushing me back on the bed. "Not up there, anyway. I just wanted to be alone with you." He pulled off his shirt, and in an instant he was lying beside me, kissing me sloppily, with his hand under my bra. After fumbling with the hook, he pushed up my shirt. I really didn't like the way he was being so rough.

"Michael," I tried to lift his head from my breasts. "Slow down. Okay? We can do this, just not so fast."

But what I said fell on drunken ears. He kissed a path down my stomach, then rolled on top of me, and with his weight pressing down on me, I could feel him swollen beneath his jeans. He tugged at my zipper.

That was it.

"No, Michael." I attempted to struggle out from under him.

He ignored what I said and managed to get my zipper down anyway. And the thing was, maybe if the circumstances had been different I wouldn't have stopped him. I liked him so much, and I had already thought it might go this far. But the circumstances weren't different. He was drunk and being way too aggressive. And anyway, this was not about us at all. It was about whatever had happened between him and his parents.

"Michael." I slapped my hand over his. "Back off!"

Moving up, breathing hard, he spoke quietly in my ear, "Come on, Rach. Don't you want this too?"

This time, I was able to push him off and get out from under him. I sat on the edge of the bed.

"Yeah, maybe I do. But not like this. Not when you're so pushy and wasted like this."

That seemed to wake him up. And for half a second he remained propped on his elbow. Then he groaned and lay heavily on his back.

I was so mad and so upset with him that I started to cry. I fastened my bra and began to straighten out my clothes. "I'm going to go home."

"Don't," Michael said, grabbing hold of my wrist as I tried to stand. There was a small, uncomfortable intermission, but a second later I felt his hand, gentle now, on my back. "I'm sorry," he said. He pulled himself up and sat next to me. "God, I am really sorry.

That was such a creepy way to act."

I wiped my face with a corner of the bedspread. "Yeah, it was."

He dropped his head.

"Don't be mad at me, Rachel. Okay?" He folded an arm around my shoulder, which made me flinch a little. That seemed to surprise him, and he took it away. He rubbed his forehead. "I am so sorry. You just have to believe me."

He was beginning to sound like the Michael I knew. And when I looked at him to see if he was, I saw that he had this amazed expression on his face, like he couldn't believe what he had just done.

"Are you really?"

He quietly nodded, took my hand in his and kissed my palm.

"Okay, let's go back to the party for a while."

"Yeah, okay."

I handed him his shirt. It was inside out, and he had trouble with it, so I took it back and turned it the right way. Once he had it on, I used my fingers to brush through his curls.

It bothered him for the rest of the summer that he had upset me that night, although I think the fact that he had upset me was all he did remember about what happened between us. As far as I was concerned that was the right thing to remember.

■ ■ ■

It was later, when we were sitting in the back yard and after Michael had played a game of poker with Cory, that I noticed him getting edgy. He hadn't had any more to drink. He just seemed unusually restless, like he needed to do something but every time he stood up to do it, he couldn't remember what it was. When he sat down for the last time, he and Cory began flicking poker chips at each other. I watched his eyes wander across the back alley to where a trail bike was parked behind Simon's neighbor's garage.

"Hey," he said, getting to his feet again after flipping the last poker chip, which landed in Cory's glass. "Let's put Brice's motorcycle on his garage."

We all looked at him because this could not have possibly come out of our conversation. Taylor and Cory had been talking about what level they'd got to in Diablo II. Anna and Sylvie had been riding them, wondering why anyone would want to play such a gruesome computer game.

Mr. Brice was the principal of Agatha and District Secondary School, and it was his garage and trail bike that were on the other side of the alley.

Anna screwed up her face. "Why?"

"What else are we doing?"

For a moment the question hung in the air. Then Sylvie laughed, because Michael was standing there like this particular idea ranked up there with the theory of relativity.

But Scott knew he meant it and so did I.

"No," said Scott.

"Why?"

"Because it's a dumb idea."

"No, it isn't," Cory disagreed. But then, he disagreed with anything Scott said. If Scott had said that the moon was round, Cory would have argued that it was square. After fishing the poker chip out of his beer, he swallowed the rest in a mouthful. "I think it's a great idea. Let's do it." It wasn't a suggestion anymore, but a challenge.

Taylor and Simon immediately agreed.

"Come on, Scott," Michael persisted. "Brice'll get home from his holidays, open the blinds and see it sitting up there on the roof. Can you imagine the look on his face? It'll be funny."

I wondered why he wasn't smiling if he really thought it was funny.

"Michael," I said, "what if something happens to it? What if you crack it up somehow?"

He saw no chance of that happening. "I won't. Scott, are you coming?"

I guess Scott knew Michael would put the motorcycle on the garage whether he agreed to it or not, because he got up and they all followed Michael across the yard. Sylvie and I walked behind them, while Anna tried to talk them out of it all the way to the garage.

"This is stupid. It's not worth it. What are you guys trying to prove?"

"Be quiet," said Cory. "Or go back in the house."

"I don't get this," I whispered to Anna.

"That makes two of us."

Which wasn't very comforting. I trusted Anna to explain to me the motives behind whatever these guys did. She'd been hanging around with them long enough, after all. But she didn't know what had possessed Michael, although she did tell me that Mr. Brice loved his trail bike. Mrs. Brice had bought it for him five years ago when he turned forty.

"He rides it around the back roads or down to Lethbridge for the day. Or to Brooks or Drumheller. But hardly ever to school."

"That's because he doesn't trust guys like Cory and Taylor," said Sylvie. "But Michael? Something very strange is going on."

It was an old garage with a flat roof, mossy sides and it was only about eight feet high. The motorcycle was parked beside it. Cory pulled the cover off and threw it on the grass. Michael and Cory walked silently around it. We were all silent because even though Mr. Brice was on holidays, there were other house lights still on. Scott and Simon watched while Michael and Cory quietly discussed how to get it up on the roof. Taylor sat on the bike and played with the gears.

"Get off," Cory told him. Releasing the kickstand, he rolled the bike through the alley to the side of the garage. "Okay, we'll do it this way. Simon, you and Taylor and Michael lift it, and Scott and I will get on the roof."

But Scott just stood right where he was and said, "No."

"All right. Simon and Taylor, you lift it. Michael and I will get on the roof. We don't need Cardinal."

Cory and Michael quietly flipped over garbage cans and climbed onto the roof. They crouched down low, waiting for the others to lift the bike. Even though it was a small bike they could hardly do it. Especially not over their shoulders. They were in danger of dropping it when Taylor yelped in a loud whisper, "Simon, let your end down!" They set it on the road again.

"This is not going to work," Simon told them.

"No kidding," said Taylor, shaking his arm.

"Let's forget it."

"Good idea," added Sylvie.

Even Cory frowned.

Michael looked impatiently at all of them. "No." He bounced from the roof of the garage down to the alley. "Simon, I'm going to get that rope ladder from your garage. We'll haul it up." He crossed the alley, carefully raised Fergusons' old garage door and disappeared inside.

Minutes later, Michael came out carrying a long, nylon rope ladder. He muttered something about Simon's dad keeping it in case of an emergency when they lived over the Fish and Chip Shop. He slipped one end through the frame of the bike and brought the two ends together so that when it was off the ground, the motorcycle would hang like it was in a sling. Cory and Michael climbed back on the roof.

"Give me the ends," Michael told Taylor.

Taylor did what he asked. And while Taylor and

Simon guided it, Michael and Cory walked backwards, pulling hard on the rope.

Anna, Sylvie and I watched the motorcycle dangle in the air. We whispered loudly for them to lower it. They ignored us.

Michael and Cory continued to tug the bike over the edge and onto the roof. Rubber scraped against asphalt. Michael told Cory to stop. Straining to hold the bike, he looked down at Scott.

"Scott, I need your help."

But Scott only looked back at him. He didn't move.

"Come on, I don't want to wreck it. You know that's not the point."

Whatever the point was, it was apparent to all of us that Michael was not going to give up.

Finally, Scott shook his head and walked over to the garbage cans, which he positioned beneath the motorcycle.

"Simon, get up on this."

Simon climbed up on one while Scott hopped on the other.

"Whoa — Cory! Wait! Not until they're ready!" Michael spluttered as he tried not to shout.

It was too late. Cory had given one more good hard wrench on the rope — it slipped and the motorcycle fell, narrowly missing Simon, who leapt out of the way just in time. The headlight smashed and the rearview mirror cracked as the bike hit the ground front first. We heard the grate of metal as it skidded across the cement.

"Cory, you wrecked it!" Sylvie shrieked. She then quickly slapped a hand across her mouth when we all hissed, "Shhh!"

Our eyes followed the small river of gasoline that bled across the driveway and trickled into the grass. Scott groaned and stepped down from the garbage can. Michael climbed down from the garage and stood next to the bike, staring at it in disbelief.

Cory jumped to the grass next to where Taylor stood. After studying the crippled bike, he glared at Michael.

"What an incredibly stupid idea," he said in a sober voice. He kicked the handlebars and walked back into Simon's house. Taylor and Simon followed him in.

Anna and I helped Scott prop the bike up against a back wall, then gathered up the broken pieces of mirror and deposited them next to the garage. Sylvie announced she was going home. Looking around, I saw Michael heading down the alley. The rest of us caught up to him. Together we walked through alleys for several blocks until we came out near the train station. No one said much as we walked. Except Michael. He had very good reasons for putting the motorcycle up on the garage. Mr. Brice deserved it for everything he'd done to him. For forcing Michael to re-write exams last year because he knew he could do better than just pass. For not letting him drop the basketball team, even though Michael told him there were other qualified guys. He deserved it for embarrassing him in front of his friends by inviting him to his house for dinner.

But mostly he deserved it for standing up at his brother's funeral and telling everybody that the deaths were a hard and a sad lesson.

"A lesson? He makes my brother getting killed into some kind of stupid lesson?!"

"Hey," Scott caught him by the arm. "Let it go."

The way Scott said it made me think they'd been through the same conversation before.

Michael only bounced his foot off the chain link fence in front of the railroad station.

Scott pressed him. "Okay?"

"Yeah, yeah, okay." He pushed Scott's arm away and continued walking.

By the time we'd crossed the track and walked another three blocks, Michael wasn't talking anymore. He wasn't even walking with us, but several feet in front of us. I wanted to catch up to him, but it was like he'd sprouted invisible quills to keep me away. He was so drawn into himself, so intense, I knew that no matter what I said I couldn't get past that. Not while he was wrestling with everything that had happened that night and whatever it was that had set it off.

We reached the intersection where he needed to take a different street than us to go home. By then we weren't very far behind him. He paused beneath a streetlight.

"See you tomorrow, Michael," I called out, hopefully.

He only briefly lifted a hand.

Scott jogged up to him. "Mike, you okay?"

Michael turned around.

"I would be. If I didn't have to go home." The light fell away from him, but I could see he was looking at me. "You know it wasn't supposed to get wrecked," he told Scott.

"Yeah, I know. But it did. Let's forget it for now. You're okay?"

I waved a couple of fingers and smiled a bit. Michael punched Scott's shoulder.

"Yeah, sure. I'm okay. I'll see you guys tomorrow." He walked toward home.

■ ■ ■

"How was the party?" Uncle Colin had been working late and was sitting in the kitchen, eating a sandwich, when I got home. Late in the afternoon, he'd operated on Bradley MacPherson's cocker spaniel. She'd had a blood blister in her ear and Uncle Colin had trouble getting the bleeding under control. He'd stayed at the clinic until he was sure she was going to be okay.

"Not bad." I poured myself a glass of juice and sat across from him.

"Want a sandwich?"

"No, thanks." I twisted a piece of my hair.

Uncle Colin took another bite of his sandwich.

"A piece of cake?" he said through a mouthful. "There's still some of that chocolate pecan Sandy made last night."

I shook my head, no.

"You're sure? I'm giving you the opportunity to get to it before I do." He winked.

I shook my head again and continued to twist my hair. It got caught in my watch and I had to rip it out.

"Is something bothering you, Rachel?"

Well, since he asked, yes, something was bothering me. Besides what had happened between me and Michael, which I hardly wanted to discuss, there was the fact that I had just witnessed a criminal activity and done nothing about it, which, when I thought about it, made me an accessory to the crime. I didn't know if I should tell him or what I should do, but I did know that I sure didn't want to get found out later and spend the next twenty years of my life in prison. I imagined myself sitting on a crude cafeteria bench, struggling to get a spoonful of gruel to my mouth, squeezed between two women with names like Sparky and Gus —

"Uncle Colin," I began, "there's something I —"

He interrupted me by holding up a hand. "Listen, Rachel, I know Agatha takes a little getting used to. The pace is certainly slower than you'd be used to and we don't have the entertainment. But I do want you to enjoy your stay while you're here. Is there anything we can do to make it better for you?"

That was the thing. Uncle Colin was such a nice guy, I *couldn't* tell him.

"No, no," I said, clearing away the dishes. "Everything's going great. I like the slow pace and I can live without the entertainment. I'm having a really good time."

SEVEN

For the next few days, Michael was in denial. He would not talk about the motorcycle incident and he immediately cut off anybody who tried. Scott, Anna and I didn't push him. I guess it was because destroying the motorcycle was so *not* like Michael that we knew he would have to get used to the idea that he'd actually done it. He would have to admit it to himself before he could admit it out loud. So when Constable Rutledge started asking questions of the people who had been at the party, we didn't exactly lie to him, we just played ignorant, hoping that Michael would eventually go talk to him on his own.

Mom and Dad came down from Yellowknife to visit the weekend following Simon's party. Mom wanted me to go shopping and she wanted to eat at Dot's Diner and Ferguson's Fish and Chip Shop and the Pink Lantern and —

"Mom, there aren't that many restaurants here."

"It doesn't matter. I just want to get out."

We went to a movie on Friday night and on Saturday afternoon we even went to a play put on by the Friends of the Library. It was about the early settlers in Agatha and the hardships they came up against and how it was only through their hard work and perseverance and cooperation that, in the end, they were able to survive. Anyway, I think that's what it was about. I do know it was very long.

"That was great!" said Mom as we emerged from the musty old fire hall. Squinting into the blinding sun, we both donned sunglasses.

"No, it wasn't." There had been another freak thunderstorm while we were in the theater and I sidestepped a stray puddle. "It was boring and it was way too long."

"Well, okay, so it wasn't great. But it beats sitting in a motel room on the edge of Yellowknife while your dad's working."

I laughed. "Oh, so that's what this is all about. Not much of an adventure?"

Mom smiled. "Maybe not. But I'm not going to complain. Your dad needs the company, Rachel. He's tired of being away from home so much. To be honest, he would never have taken the job in Yellowknife if he'd had a choice."

"Then why was he trying to make it sound like such a terrific deal?"

"So you would think it was."

Something was getting to Mom. She's usually a pretty positive person and to her credit, she rarely uses the guilt thing unless she's tired and can't think of anything else.

Aunt Sandy was making a feast for dinner when Mom and I got back to the house. Dad and Uncle Colin had just returned from Cypress Hills, where they'd been fishing for the day. Aunt Sandy hustled me out of the kitchen when I offered to peel the carrots.

"Out of here, Rachel. You should go visit with your dad."

Yeah, yeah, I should. But —

"— I'm real good at making little carrot curls by chilling them in water."

"That may be so," she said, prying the vegetable peeler from my hand. "But he's going to think you don't want to talk to him."

"Do ya think?"

Plunking her hands on her hips, she frowned at me.

"Oh, all right. If you insist."

So I sat down in the living room, waiting to see if Dad had grown any more civil in the time that he had been away. He asked me the questions I was expecting: What did I do at the clinic? Had I made any friends? And very predictably — was I behaving myself?

I stalled for a moment before answering. It was important that I come up with the perfect words. The answers that were generic enough that he wouldn't overreact and, therefore, cause me a lot of stress. Okay, I feed and walk the dogs. Yes, I'd made friends. And, absolutely, I was behaving. I then thought about adding, "When was the last time you were woken up at four in the morning by the police?" On second thought, there was no point provoking him. But I had no sooner opened my mouth to answer than Uncle Colin must have decided that I needed his help.

"I'm telling you, Al, we've been so busy this summer, I don't know what we'd have done without Rachel. And yes, she's made friends. Lots of them. As a matter of fact," he winked at me, "I think there may even be a certain young man."

Oh great! Way to destroy the whole evening! I knew exactly how Dad would react to that — like Troy Atkinson was on the phone. Digging my toes in the carpet, getting ready to defend myself, I turned to face him. I was surprised to see that he wasn't even looking at me, but instead, he was staring into his drink.

"A young man," he repeated absently. "Well, that's just fine."

Huh? I couldn't believe it. No rash, illogical comment dragged from the Dark Ages? From Dad? It was almost scary.

"It is?"

Dad looked up. "Sorry, Rachel. I guess my mind wandered for a minute. Did someone say it's time to eat?"

I was still puzzling over this when the doorbell rang. I got up to answer it. It was Anna, standing on the step with a real urgent look on her face.

"Come with me," she whispered. "Me and Sylvie. We're going over to Rib Bone's cabin. You've got to come with us."

"Why?"

"Rib Bone is up to something."

I glanced back to the living room. Dad was now listening to Uncle Colin, who was standing up tall, demonstrating the size of the moose he'd seen in the bush down in Spruce Coulee. I asked Aunt Sandy how long dinner would be.

"About an hour."

"Is it all right if I go out with Anna for a bit?"

"Of course."

Anna had borrowed her mom's car. It was only the second time she'd driven on her own since getting her license, and after driving with her for a block, I wondered how she had ever pulled it off.

The car was parked facing the wrong direction on Uncle Colin's side of the street with a back wheel up on the sidewalk. Sylvie was in the passenger seat, so I jumped in the back. Anna turned the key in the ignition and shifted the gear into first. We lurched forward a couple of times and the car stalled.

"That wasn't very smooth," said Sylvie.

Anna made a face at her and started the car again. This time we only lurched once before we began moving slowly forward. Anna shifted gears and we drove to the end of the street. She was halfway through the intersection before we came to a stop.

"You missed the stop sign!" Sylvie squealed.

"I didn't miss it. It's just back there a bit."

"Anna!" Sylvie twisted her head back and forth to see if there were any cars in our path. "If someone had been flying through we could have been killed!"

"Shut up, Sylvie. If I'd wanted a critic, I would have invited my mom to come along." A grinding sound came from the engine as Anna tried to shift gears. She finally got it in place, started forward and stalled the car again.

Sylvie groaned, which only made Anna madder.

"Look, you have no idea how many things there are to do at once — forget all the stupid signs!"

This time Sylvie did shut up. I figured she was probably thinking the same thing as me. If we harassed her too much, Anna would just get more frustrated, make another dumb move and kill us all. We didn't say a word while Anna turned the corner and chugged up Exhibition Road.

"Okay, so what's up?" I asked once she had parked the car and we were safely walking down the railroad tracks.

She told me she'd bumped into Cory and Taylor that afternoon. They'd been by Rib Bone's cabin when they were cutting across Rasmussen's land.

"They said Rib Bone's been digging a big hole."

The *way* she said it was like there was some kind of significance in this.

"Yeah, and? He's probably planting another garden."

"No, it's a grave. Cory told me it's about the size of Megan Gillis."

"About the size of Megan Gillis," I repeated.

Sylvie giggled. "Anna, of course Cory would tell you that! That's just like him."

"Yes, but I'm sure he's right. Think about it. Rib Bone's a known murderer. Megan's been missing for two weeks. Rib Bone has a fresh grave on his property. It all makes perfect sense!"

"Uh-huh. Well, I guess if you say so, it does."

We passed Mr. Potter, who was brightening the pavilion with a coat of white paint. We jogged across the ties.

"Anna, just what are *we* going to do?" I jumped to the side of the track where the gravel crunched beneath my feet.

"We're going to confirm my suspicions are true."

"How?"

"We're going to sneak up to Rib Bone's cabin and see what he's up to."

"Whoa!" I stopped. "You mean while he's at home? Do you really think that's such a good plan? I mean, if he *is* a murderer."

"He won't even know we're there."

Finally, we reached the end of O'Conner's land. We climbed the fence and continued to jog along the railroad tracks until we came to the train trestle.

"Come on," said Anna, jogging right onto it.

Sylvie turned to see if I was actually following them.

I did follow, although I was careful that with each step I placed my foot squarely on a tie. We crept up the hill. Anna stubbed her toe on a rock and I scratched my bare ankle on a coarse shrub. We snuck around to the front of the cabin, where we lay on our stomachs behind the big rock. We could see Rib Bone Squire sitting on a low stool.

He was working, sanding the roof of a small birdhouse. He wore denim overalls that were too short for him and a red cardigan, even though it was a very hot day. His head was down as he stroked the sandpaper across the wood. I'm still not sure if it was the way he kept bringing his sleeve up to rub the dust from his eyes, or the fact that his mind seemed to be somewhere else, but it struck me that he looked very tired.

I searched the yard for the grave Anna had described. It was just to the side of the house. And it *was* a grave. I knew this because there was a marker planted at one end of it. I had to believe Anna then.

I glanced at Anna, who had turned pale. She let out a gasp. Rib Bone stopped sanding and looked up. Clamping a hand to her mouth, Anna yanked my arm hard, so hard that I was almost surprised my body went with it. I yanked Sylvie and the three of us ran back toward the hill. We stumbled through the grass and scrambled down the hill and pounded over the train trestle as fast as we could go.

"It was Megan Gillis!" Anna exclaimed. "What did I tell you?"

"Anna," I said, trying to grasp my breath. We jogged up to O'Connor's field, slipping now on the long grass which was still a little damp. "We can't be sure."

"Yes, Rachel, we can. Who else would be buried there? What I can't believe is that this time he buried the body right next to his house!"

We leaned against the fence, breathing hard.

"Rachel, what are we going to do? We need to tell someone he did it. Someone who will believe us."

"What about your mom and dad?"

She shook her head. "They won't listen. They never listen to anything I say."

Sylvie perked up. "I know. What about your Uncle Colin?"

Yeah, Uncle Colin would be okay. He maybe wouldn't believe us — I mean, if there was anything to believe — but he would certainly listen.

Anna quickly agreed. "Dr. Bennett. Good plan. Okay, let's go back to Rachel's house."

We started off again. We were about halfway back to the exhibition grounds when it struck me just how obvious the whole thing was.

"Hey, wait a minute!" I stopped in the middle of the tracks. "Where was his dog? Anna, I didn't see his dog. That must have been old Watson. Poor old Watson must have died!"

And, as I found out later that evening, he had. Watson was the reason Uncle Colin had been called to the clinic at eight o'clock the night before.

Anna and Sylvie stopped on the tracks ahead of me.

"Remember, his golden retriever?" I waved my hand frantically in the direction of the coulee.

"Nope." Anna started walking again. "It wasn't his dog."

But Sylvie didn't take any more convincing. She looked at me and shrugged. She caught up to Anna. "Anna, Rachel's right. Of course it was Watson."

Anna brushed Sylvie away. And perhaps because she was embarrassed — because she had believed something that was so transparent to the rest of us — she didn't say anything else until we were in the car and driving down Exhibition Road.

"Okay," she finally agreed, flipping a hand, "maybe it was his dog."

She said it at the exact same moment Mr. Brice stepped out into the intersection at the bottom of the hill.

"Anna!" Sylvie and I both shrieked.

And in one heart-paralyzing instant, Mr. Brice leapt backwards to the sidewalk, where he sat down hard on the curb. Anna screeched to a stop and thank goodness for seat belts is all I can say.

"Oh, my god! I ran over Mr. Brice!"

We tore after Anna as she flew out of the car and rushed over to help him.

"Mr. Brice! Are you all right?!" She knelt down on the asphalt next to him.

"Yes, yes, I'm all right," Mr. Brice decided, standing up, smacking dust off his butt. "But Anna, the idea is to stop *before* the sign."

"I know, I know! I'm sorry!" Anna spluttered."It's just that — I was thinking about something else!" And she was suddenly so frightened by what she'd almost done that tears filled her eyes.

Assuring her a second time that he was all right, Mr. Brice squeezed her arm. "Well, in future, if something requires that much thought, it might be wise for you to think about it when you're not driving a car."

Anna wiped her face with her hand and nodded. "I'm s*oo* sorry. I'll be more careful. Are you sure you're okay? Can you walk?"

Mr. Brice waggled one leg and then the other before stepping from the curb. "Yes, I think I probably can. It might be a while before I break any pole-vaulting records though."

Anna smiled.

"So you promise me you'll pay more attention to the road?"

She promised that she would. Mr. Brice said goodbye and we watched as he started across the crosswalk. He limped ever so slightly.

"Mr. Brice," Anna called after him, "maybe I should drive you home."

I almost laughed at the suggestion.

"No, that won't be necessary." He had walked a few more feet before he brought a hand to his forehead, stopped and turned around. "You know, perhaps there *is* something you girls might be able to help me with."

"Sure, what's that?" Sylvie asked.

"Were either of you at Simon Ferguson's party a week ago?"

Anna and Sylvie quickly glanced at each other, but only Sylvie nodded.

"Well, I don't know if you know this, but my motorcycle was damaged and I thought you might have heard something or seen something that might help me find out who was responsible."

Anna dropped her eyes to the asphalt. "No, Mr. Brice, I didn't."

"All right. Sylvie, how about you?"

Sylvie took a little longer to answer, but she also avoided his eyes. "No, Mr. Brice, I didn't either."

Mr. Brice just looked at me and smiled. "Okay. Well, thank you. You're both good students and I'm only asking because I know I can trust you. All of you have a good summer, now." Mr. Brice waved, reached the other side of the crosswalk and stepped up onto the curb.

When he was well down the sidewalk, Anna kicked her mom's tire. "Those guys! They made us lie."

"Anna," said Sylvie. "We didn't have to be there."

Anna only looked at her. I guess she knew that what Sylvie said was true.

■ ■ ■

Dinner was almost ready when I got back to the house. Dad was standing next to the dining room table, chatting with Uncle Colin, who was opening a bottle of wine. Mom and Aunt Sandy were in the kitchen, arranging food on plates and serving dishes. They asked me to toss the salad. After washing my hands and moving down the counter, closer to the dining room, so they would have more room to work, I began tearing lettuce and chopping cucumbers. That's when I overheard Dad. It wasn't like I was listening in on his conversation or anything; it was simply the way it happened.

"They let two engineers go earlier this spring," he was telling Uncle Colin. "We haven't been getting the contracts. I'm worried that I may be next in line."

I stopped chopping. Carrying a basket of croissants, Aunt Sandy squeezed past me on her way to the table. I looked up to see Mom standing next to me, cradling a tomato in her hand.

"Here, Rachel. This should go in too." Her voice was almost apologetic, like it was a big deal that she hadn't given it to me earlier.

But I didn't take it. "He could have said something. It's not like we're little kids anymore. It would have been a whole lot easier on all of us if he'd told us what was going on. I mean, instead of just being in a bad mood all the time."

"He *should* have said something." Mom sighed and set the tomato on the counter. "I should have said something, but he didn't want me to. He didn't want to worry you. Or Sean, before he left for school."

"Everything's ready —" Aunt Sandy popped her head back in the kitchen, "except that salad."

Mom and I turned and looked at her like we had forgotten why we were there. Mom grabbed a knife and sliced the tomato. I returned to the cucumber. When everything was chopped, I tossed it all together and carried it into the dining room.

I didn't eat a lot that night. I didn't feel very hungry and besides, I was busy watching Dad organize the food on his plate. He had a compulsive habit which I didn't notice much anymore, but everything had its place and he ate only one thing at a time.

"Want some salad, Dad?" The dishes had made the rounds and I noticed he hadn't taken any.

Dad was pretty intent on what he was doing. He shook his head, no.

"Are you sure? I tossed it myself."

He looked up. He studied his full plate, then his side plate filled with a croissant.

"You tossed it yourself?"

I nodded.

"In that case, I'm sure I can make some room."

EIGHT

The Agatha Rodeo and Exhibition was in three weeks. Volunteers were needed so Anna, Sylvie and I met Michael and Scott at the pavilion in the fairgrounds to sign up. Anna and Sylvie had already decided that they wanted to help out in the stables, grooming the Clydesdales and champion Charolais. I still carried the paralyzing image of Boomerang barreling toward me in my head — so I opted to read to the little kids in the day care where it was safe.

Scott and Michael volunteered to help set up game booths, sawing boards and pounding nails. Simon was going to flip hamburgers in the barbecue tent with his dad. Cory and Taylor volunteered to supervise traffic in the bumper car ring. Mr. Potter looked up from his book where he was writing all this down.

"Are you sure you two are right for the job?"

I don't think Mr. Potter was so sure himself.

"Yeah, and if they don't drive properly," Taylor announced, "we'll jump in and show them how it's done."

Mr. Potter only muttered something about that's what he was afraid of. He wrote their names down in his book.

■ ■ ■

We were going fishing at Sullivan's Pond north of Agatha that morning. After leaving the pavilion, we strolled across the yard toward the stables, where we had left our fishing rods leaning against a wall. At first my heart hit my throat because Uncle Colin's rod was not where I had left it. Quickly looking around, I spotted Taylor goofing with it in the parking lot, casting at nothing in particular from where he sat on the hood of his limousine.

I bounded toward him. "Taylor! Give me that!"

He turned at the sound of my voice. He had just let the line fly again and it got tangled in a branch over his head. Laughing, he left it dangling from the tree, jumped from the hood and, spewing gravel all over the grass, drove off with Cory in the limousine.

Michael had borrowed Mr. Goodwyn's truck for the day. Once we had rescued my rod, minus several yards of line, we loaded all the fishing rods, along with our tackle boxes, in the back of the truck. I climbed up next to Michael in the front seat, and Sylvie, Anna and Scott piled into the back of the cab. Surrounded by broad windows and sitting up so high, I had a great

view as we bumped over potholes and drove down
Exhibition Road. Michael came to a stop before the
crosswalk at the bottom of the hill.

"I hope you were paying attention to that," Sylvie
said to Anna.

Michael turned the corner.

"Paying attention to what?"

"The way Michael came to a perfect stop. You know,
so that if someone like, say, Mr. Brice, were crossing
the street, he wouldn't be killed."

Anna threw a rubber worm at her across Scott's lap.

"Ooooh, yuck! Get it out!"

Scott pulled it out of her hair.

Kicking my sandals off, stretching my bare feet before me, I let the dry air rush over my face as we headed
out on the highway. We drove past a herd of grazing
bison, and even from a distance, I could see they were
shedding their heavy coats. Their shaggy brown hides
were ratty and uneven, and here and there, clumps of
hair hung from the fence like old gum. Five miles down
the highway, Michael turned onto a gravel road. We
rumbled across a cattle gate and arrived at Sullivan's
Pond. A large sign showed us how the pond had been
created when Alberta Wildlife diverted a small piece of
the South Saskatchewan River. Uncle Colin, who was
involved in the project, had helped stock it with rain-
bow trout.

Scott was the first one out of the truck. After laying
his fishing rod on the grass he squatted next to it and

opened his tackle box. His forehead creased in thought as his fingers hovered above his collection of flies.

I walked with Michael down to the edge of the pond. The shore was fringed with bulrushes and cattails, and at the one end where we stood, a wide gray dock stretched into the silky brown water, which reflected only one small cloud, the sun and us.

Michael released the clasp on his own tackle box, and after explaining to me why he was using the brown midge, he tied it to his line. He showed me how to do the same thing, snipping the excess line with his pocket-knife once I had tied the knot. Anna was well down the shore, away from us, where she was already fishing. Sylvie wasn't fishing. She was reading a book, suntanning, because she would rather catch the bubonic plague than some creepy old fish.

Michael suggested I fish from the dock. After giving me a few pointers on how to cast, he gathered his own rod and tackle box and walked further down toward Scott so we wouldn't cross lines. I cast a few times, trying to keep in mind what Michael had told me, attempting to use the motions Uncle Colin had taught me in the back yard the night before. I was still lousy at it, but I did manage to get at least a few casts past the end of the dock. Folding my legs beneath me, I sat down. A small black shape, a muskrat, emerged from the cattails and slipped from shore. Michael looked over when he heard the slap of its tail as it dove. He was about to cast again. I watched as he eased back and put his whole body into it. The sun caught the silver line as it drifted through the air. The brown midge just barely nicked the surface, then danced above the water. A fish jumped.

"Hey," said Scott. "They've finally noticed we're here."

And as if grabbed by an invisible hand, the end of Michael's fishing rod suddenly bowed down so low that it almost touched the surface of the water.

"Ha! He's got it!" he exclaimed.

I know *my* immediate reaction would have been to crank that reel hard, haul that fish in, grab it while I could. But Michael was much more patient than I. At least when it came to things he understood, which in this case was fish.

"Okay, Rachel, watch this. This is what I was telling you. Now I'm going to play him for a while. Give him lots of line. Tire him out a bit."

And he did give it lots of line. Yards and yards of line. Miles and miles it seemed! I thought that fish must have had enough to take it to the bottom of the Mariana Trench when it suddenly broke the surface right in front of me and for the first time I saw how magnificent it was. The trout arced and its silver-pink body shimmered against the sky.

Scott whistled, "Man, I'll bet you he's at least four pounds!"

Michael walked slowly down toward Scott, reeling the line in, then letting it slide. After a while, when the fish just barely struggled and Scott stood close to shore waiting to slip the net beneath it, I left my rod on the dock and went over to watch.

Scott scooped the flapping trout from the pond in a rush of water. Laying his rod aside, Michael freed it from the net and after examining it, showed me how the hook was lodged in its lower lip. He held it firmly behind the gills and very carefully extracted the hook from its delicate mouth. I told him he would make a good surgeon, because when he was finished there was not a drop of blood. He carried it to the end of the dock where he gently released it into the pond. It flipped twice and disappeared.

"Okay, Rachel. Your turn."

"All right," I said. "Just you watch."

He laughed and walked back along the shore.

We'd been fishing again for less than fifteen minutes when Cory and Taylor showed up in the limousine. They had come down to talk to Scott.

"Oh yeah?" Taking a tip from Michael, Scott was studying his tackle box again. "About what?"

"About the fact that we just got a visit from Rutledge, and Brice is accusing us of dropping his motorcycle from the roof of his garage."

Scott didn't look up. "Now why would Mr. Brice think that?"

Cory slammed the lid of Scott's tackle box shut with his foot. "That's what we thought you could tell us."

"Hey, moron. Get lost. I have no idea how he found out."

Taylor didn't say anything, but I saw his eyes scan the ground. Spotting what he wanted, he walked over to the side of the road and picked up a large rock. He carried it so that he was standing close to Anna and heaved it in the pond.

Anna jumped back. "Quit that!"

"How did he find out?" Taylor insisted.

"I don't know." Scott threw the lid of his tackle box open again. "But I know we didn't have anything to do with it. Maybe he just put two and two together."

"What's that supposed to mean?"

I watched Sylvie pull a cattail from the marshy edge. Dragging it out behind her, she wandered down the shore.

"It means," said Anna, plunking a hand on her hip, "that he must have remembered the time you pulled the fire alarm just before Finlayson's final math exam. And who could forget the day Cory rode his dirt bike through school?"

Taylor laughed. "That was so cool. Remember the look on his face when you came around the corner and nearly mowed him down?"

"Come on, Taylor, a monkey could figure out who put the motorcycle on the garage."

Cory squinted. "Yeah, well what about Michael? He's no saint. How come Brice isn't accusing him too?"

Taylor stepped forward. "Because it was one of these guys who tipped him off."

Michael, who had been trying to ignore them, reeled

in his line. After laying the fishing rod on the grass he spat on the ground. "Take off, Sparshatt. Nobody here said anything."

Taylor looked quietly at him for a moment. Then, surprisingly, he came back to the dock and spoke to me. "Hey Rachel, have you caught any fish yet?"

It was kind of an odd, rather friendly question, I mean, considering the seriousness of the conversation. The others must have thought so too because they all waited for me to answer.

"Uh, no. Not yet." I glanced over at Anna, wondering if this was the right thing to say. "But I'm not really all that good at fishing."

"Oh yeah? Well, it's really pretty easy. Here, let me show you how!"

Michael and Anna moved fast, but not as fast as Taylor, who jumped on the dock and grabbed me from behind. He clamped a thick arm around my neck and I dropped Uncle Colin's fishing rod on the dock.

"Bell," Taylor warned Michael, who was still about ten feet away from us, "*you* stay right where you are!" With his arm still around my neck, he shuffled me further out on the dock so that we were standing very close to the edge.

Michael did stop. Cory stood between him and the dock.

I looked down at the water, which did not look so silky anymore.

"Taylor," I whimpered, "I can't swim."

Which wasn't entirely true, but it was true enough. I could swim; I just really couldn't picture myself swimming in that swamp. What if my feet got stuck in the mud on the bottom and I got tangled in the reeds and I was anchored there, to be circled by muskrats for eternity!

"Come on, Sparshatt." Michael took another step toward me. "Quit fooling around."

This only prompted Taylor to force me so close to the edge that I lost my balance, and with one foot dangling above the water, I had to depend on him to pull me back.

"Taylor!"

When he did pull me back, I kicked his shin hard, which only made him laugh.

Scott pushed between Cory and Michael. "Sparshatt. She can't swim. Let her go."

"When you tell us who squealed."

"We already told you, dickhead — it wasn't us!"

I really did appreciate Michael sticking up for me, but I wished that he would hold off on the insults until I was on safer ground. I dug my heel hard into Taylor's big shoe. He didn't even wince. Cory only watched. He didn't say anything until Michael tried to push past him.

"Don't give him a reason to do it," he warned.

Which made me wonder whose side he was really on.

Taylor wrapped his arm tighter around my neck. The big goon! He spoke to Scott again. "Well? What did you say?"

"Taylor?" Sylvie was back, still dragging the cattail

out behind her. "Let Rachel go. It wasn't any of them. It was me."

She was so calm and quiet about it that we didn't immediately believe her. She dropped the cattail and phrased it another way.

"I told Mr. Brice."

We all just looked at her.

Taylor let his arm drop from my neck, which gave me a moment to scramble off the dock and get close to Michael.

But Anna wanted to be sure. "You told Mr. Brice what, Sylvie?"

"That these guys dropped the motorcycle from the garage."

"Sylvie — why?"

"Because, Anna, I would never have passed science if he hadn't helped me. Because he explained stuff over again to me after school and he was always so nice about it and he didn't make me feel stupid. I told him because he told *me* I was a good student. And then I lied. Right to his face."

There was really nothing else to be said. That was how Sylvie felt and that's why she'd done it and now it was obviously too late to talk her out of it.

Cory kicked the dock and swore. He headed back toward the limousine. Taylor started to follow. I think he had already forgotten what a creep he had been. Which made him an easy target for Michael and Scott, who hadn't forgotten. Michael cuffed him on the side of the head as he walked off the dock. Taylor slumped a bit. He made a move to swing back, but Scott caught him in the stomach. Realizing he faced both Michael and Scott with no back-up, he held up his hands. Michael and Scott let him pass as he followed Cory to the limousine.

Anna threw a handful of grass after him. "Someone should put a leash on that guy!"

"Forget it," Scott waved it all aside with his fishing rod. "Come on, Mike. Let's walk further down. I saw a couple of big ones jump."

"You okay?" Michael asked me.

I nodded.

He picked up his rod and wandered further down the shore with Scott. Anna had already retrieved her fishing rod from where she had dropped it in the grass. She was moaning at the sight of the tangled line. I knelt down on the grass to help her untangle it.

"Anna?" Sylvie's shadow fell over us. "Are you mad?"

Anna looked up for a moment. Without saying anything, she cut the tangled piece off her line. She folded the knife and stuffed it in her pocket. She spoke to me.

"Mr. Brice helped me build a model of a solar-heated house for the science fair. Remember that, Sylvie? And you know what, Rachel ... I won."

NINE

"Know how you get rid of a tapeworm?" Michael slapped his paintbrush back and forth across the school fence.

"No," said Anna, carefully dabbing her brush between the boards. "And I don't want to know."

"Well, that's too bad. Because I'm going to tell you anyway." Michael stopped to dip his brush in the paint can. "You eat a donut every day at the same time for a week, then you stop. After a couple of days that tapeworm comes up from your stomach, looking for its sugar fix. You grab it by the head and you pull it out."

"Ooooh!" Dropping our paintbrushes to our sides, Anna and I clapped our hands across our mouths.

Scott kind of laughed.

"Michael, that is so gross. You're gross! You didn't have to tell us that!" squawked Anna.

"Hey, I didn't make it up! Did I, Scott? Popowich told us that in biology last year. Besides, I was just trying to make Rachel feel better."

I raised my eyebrows. "How?"

"Well, there are a lot worse things than swimming in muddy ponds with muskrats."

I waited for him to finish so that what he said would make some sense, but Michael didn't say anything else, so I said, "That's supposed to make me feel better?"

"Well — yeah." He was grinning at me.

I painted the tip of his nose. I liked Michael a lot, but I have to admit, sometimes I just don't get guys. I mean, the weird way they think.

We were painting the fence that ran around Agatha and District Secondary School. Scott and Michael had to do it. They'd been doing it for the past two days. Empty paint cans lay scattered in the grass all along the fence that separated the school yard from the parking lot. Cory and Taylor and Simon also had to do it. They were on the other side of the field. Sylvie was doing it because she felt responsible since she was the one who had squealed to Mr. Brice. Anna and I had been helping out for the last hour because we'd been all over Agatha and we were bored.

When Mr. Brice pulled up to the curb, Michael was still chuckling at making Anna sick over his tapeworm story. It surprised me how serious he got so quickly. I watched him watch Mr. Brice get out of his car. And, as Mr. Brice walked across the field toward us, Michael turned his back on him.

"Well, boys — and gals," Mr. Brice added when he

saw Anna and Sylvie and me helping out. "Another hour and you should be done." He strolled next to the fence, looking up and down, checking out our work, "And I must say, you're doing a super job. Oops!" Pausing about ten feet away from us, he turned a finger in a circle, pointing out a bald spot that had been missed. "Michael, there's a patch that got missed here, son."

I had met Mr. Brice only the one time when Anna almost ran over him. And I had thought then that he seemed like a decent guy. So I was pretty sure that he wasn't pointing out the missed spot to be critical. He really did seem to be *only* pointing it out. But when he said it, Michael's shoulders tightened and he went right on painting as if he hadn't heard Mr. Brice.

"Michael?"

Scott stopped painting.

"Did you hear me? There's a spot that got missed here."

Michael still didn't look up or make any effort to fix the bald spot. "Yeah, all right," was all he said.

Scott scrambled up from his knees. "I'll get that." He squashed his paintbrush into the bottom of the paint can and quickly painted over the spot Mr. Brice was pointing at.

Mr. Brice dropped his arm. "All right. Thank you, Scott. That looks just fine. I'm going to see how the other boys are doing." He walked back along the fence, laying his hand on Michael's shoulder as he passed, giving a friendly squeeze.

Sylvie began lecturing Michael as soon as Mr. Brice was across the field. "You shouldn't just ignore him like that, Michael. It's not like he ever did anything to you."

I didn't really agree with the blunt way she said it, but in a way Sylvie was right. Michael hadn't been very polite — at least, not for someone who usually was.

Anna tossed her a warning look, telling her to shhh.

Michael didn't immediately react. He just smacked his paintbrush against the fence, back and forth and up and down again.

"He shouldn't call me son."

"He's only trying to be nice to you. He's *always* trying to be nice to you."

This time, Anna leaned over and grabbed Sylvie by the arm. "Leave it alone."

Sylvie shook her loose. She was mad at Michael, and she wouldn't leave it alone. "Michael, you've got a real problem and you shouldn't take it out on Mr. Brice. He shouldn't call you son. He shouldn't look at you. He shouldn't tell you what to do!"

"Sylvie, take a pill!"

"No, Anna." Sylvie jumped to her feet. "Don't any of you get it? We wouldn't even be doing this if it wasn't for Michael."

Scott told her to drop it. He told her — he almost insisted — that it wasn't such a big deal.

But Sylvie wouldn't drop it, and I realized from what she said next that this was probably because it was something she'd been thinking about for a very long time.

"Michael, you've got to stop blaming everybody else for Nick's death. Mr. Brice had nothing to do with it. If you'd just talk about it maybe you would finally figure that out. Quit blaming him. Quit blaming everybody else!"

Michael glared at her for a few seconds. He didn't say anything to her, but he picked up the empty paint can and slammed it hard against the fence. He slammed two more empty cans against the fence as he started down the length of the field.

"You're wrong," Anna told Sylvie. "Some things are better left not said. Some things just hurt too much. If Michael wants to talk about Nick it's up to him, it's not up to you to decide."

I couldn't believe what had just happened. What had started out as a great day had just been destroyed with a few careless words. I tore after Michael.

"Michael!"

He didn't answer me.

"Michael! She shouldn't have said that." I caught up to him, but his whole body told me not to come any closer than I was. He kicked another empty paint can.

"She didn't mean to offend you." I skipped behind him. "Michael, listen to me. I'm sure Sylvie didn't mean it the way it came out."

"Rachel, leave me alone."

"No, come on. Talk to me."

He whirled around on me. And at that moment I stopped talking because I suddenly knew that nothing I said was going to make any difference. Not when I could see the sadness that he struggled against, so vivid now, in his dark eyes. His voice was solemn and steady when he spoke to me again.

"Stay here. Okay? I mean it. I want you to leave me alone."

It hurt so much to hear it, but I did as he asked and I didn't follow when he started walking again. Anna and Scott caught up with me. Scott went after him, but he got the same reaction that I did. Coming back to where I stood by the fence, he tried to convince me that Michael would be over it in a couple of hours.

■ ■ ■

But he wasn't over it in a couple of hours. We waited for him to call and we went over to his house, but he wasn't there. We walked through town, hoping to find him at Dot's or maybe hanging around Rotary Park. Scott called Goodwyn's farm, but Mrs. Goodwyn hadn't seen him all day. Late in the afternoon, Scott borrowed his dad's car and we drove around Agatha looking for him. We checked out the train station and hiked out to the cave after going through the buildings on the exhibition grounds. We drove to Palliser Point, where Scott and I walked among the twisted cottonwoods and Anna and Sylvie followed the path along the river. We even drove out to Sullivan's Pond.

As we were driving back into town, we tried to make sense of what had happened so fast. We tried to analyze the way Michael thought and predict where he might go. A thundercloud burst and the highway became slick. Rain beat against the windshield and Sylvie confessed that she could just kick herself for opening her big mouth. None of us disagreed. She told us that she had only been trying to help him, and, in her own way, I guess we all knew that she probably had.

Early in the evening, Mrs. Bell phoned Scott and me because Michael hadn't shown up for dinner. She was becoming a little concerned. Both Scott and Anna's parents needed their cars, so we rode our bikes back up to the exhibition grounds. We walked through the pavilion once more. We checked the stables, and, while Anna and Scott combed the grandstand and the bleachers, I hurried back to the field of fireweed Michael had rushed me out of the clinic to show me the day before.

"I want you to hear something," he'd told me, as we'd climbed into Mr. Goodwyn's truck, "but we've got to get there by one o'clock."

"Get where?"

"To the field on the other side of the pavilion."

"Why, what's up there?"

"Fireweed. Half an acre of it."

"Michael," I'd said as we bumped up Exhibition Road, "you want me to *hear* a field of weeds?"

"You got it."

Michael parked the truck and I'd followed him around to the back of the pavilion. Holding stray branches from my face, he'd led me through the tangled grass and wild rose bushes to where the prairie opened up again on the other side. Just before it did was the field of fireweed. The tall purple stalks stood straight in the distance. There was no wind to disturb them except maybe the tiniest whisper stirred up by a butterfly as it settled on a leaf. The whole scene was certainly wonderful to look at, the millions of flower petals like a silent explosion of mauve against the sky, but I was supposed to be hearing something. Taking my hand, Michael stepped quietly forward again.

"Now listen," he'd said, standing barely as tall as the nearest stalk.

But he didn't need to tell me to what, because the hum had already reached my ears. The flat, solid drone whirled up from the field with the ferocity of an approaching tornado. I didn't know whether I should run for my life or take a chance and experience something I'd never seen. It was bees. Thousands — probably hundreds of thousands of them! It was the weirdest thing, the clamor of so many insects, like the scariest ride on the midway, frightening, yet totally mesmerizing at the same time.

"Why are they here?" I'd whispered to Michael, as if my voice could possibly disturb them. As if the entire mob would care enough to stop what they were doing and ask, "Who's she?"

"Nectar. They know that one o'clock is the fireweed's most productive time."

"Incredible. I mean that they would figure that out." Sitting down in the grass, I'd leaned back against Michael.

"Not really. They've only learned the best way to survive."

■　■　■

But now there was nothing in the field except the fireweed and a few loitering bees. Michael seemed to have simply disappeared.

After meeting back in front of the grandstand, Scott suggested riding out to the cave one more time. Again, Michael wasn't there. We had run out of ideas, and with fear weighing heavily in my stomach, I sank into a chair. Anna slouched in the chair across from me while Scott paced up and down, thinking. And except for the soft drone of the South Saskatchewan River flowing through Buffalo Coulee below us, and me sniffing now and again, there was no other sound. Until Scott said, "Wait a minute! I think I know where he might be."

"Where?"

"Abbott's. Come on, let's get our bikes."

We grabbed our bikes from where we'd left them in the sand and, stumbling with them, made our way down through Buffalo Coulee. We followed the path that ran next to the river, riding where the stubby old willows didn't prevent us, steering our bikes over the flat dry grass when they became too thick to get through. We sped across the gray surface of Palliser Point Park, through the gate and onto the highway. The sun was low and a soft orange glow illuminated the sky. With Scott way ahead of us, we pedaled into it for what seemed like at least a mile. Scott turned down Gravel Pit Road. Just past a clump of trees, before the gravel pit, I saw a small faded sign in the grass, "Abbott's Go-Karts." We rode behind Scott down the bumpy lane that led to the go-cart track.

Abbott's Go-Karts looked like it had not been in business for quite some time. The bleachers sagged and leaned to one side, and the paint on the small concession stand was peeling in long pink strips. There was only one go-cart that I could see. It was off to the side, back by a garage that was sinking into the ground. It was almost hidden in the long yellow grass. Scott had already found it, but I guess he knew it was there. Michael was sitting in it.

We dropped our bikes in the dirt. Anna and I walked behind Scott across the racetrack. Scott adjusted his baseball cap as he stood next to the go-cart. Michael didn't even look at us or seem to notice that we were there. He just kept staring at the track like there was a private race going on that we weren't privileged enough to see.

"Hey," said Scott.

"Hey," said Michael.

We sat down next to him in the grass. Scott gave

Michael a little shove on the shoulder. "We've been looking for you."

Michael still didn't look at us. He just said, "Yeah, well, it looks like you found me."

"I thought you might be here." Scott gazed at the abandoned track, all blown over with tumbleweeds. They'd brought the go-cart from Michael's house earlier in the spring, he told me later. They'd hidden it in the old garage, planning to work on it when they had time.

Scott leaned over Michael and turned the steering wheel, which was attached to a long rod. The front wheels creaked as they ground against the gravel, and grasshoppers flew from the front end. A rusty nut dropped from the axle.

"Looks like we could still get it going." He picked up the nut. "With a little elbow grease."

"Nick built things to last."

"Yeah, I know. Nick was good at that. He could build pretty much anything. How's the engine?"

I noticed the tool kit which lay open in the grass. "It started."

"Yeah? After sitting in your garage all this time?"

"I had to coax it a little."

Scott tipped his hat. "Nick would be real glad." He leaned back on his elbows and grinned. "Remember the fort he helped us build down in the ravine behind your house?"

Michael batted a mosquito from his arm. "Yeah."

"It was so sweet. He even wired it. Your dad nearly

had a heart attack when he saw all the cords running from the house down to the woods, but it worked and nobody was electrocuted, and we had lights and we could run a fan and a radio and the popcorn maker."

Michael kind of laughed.

"Hey, remember when he built that raft? You should have seen us," Scott said to Anna and me. "What were we — about seven? Nick must have been eleven. He'd worked on that raft all summer. He took us for a ride down the river like he was Huck Finn. He was so proud and we were lying in the front on our stomachs, dragging our hands through the water while Nick pushed us along next to the bank with a big pole. We was goin' down the Mississippi River, which would fetch us all the way to Armstrong's Stables. Then it started raining. Mike and me were laughing, killing ourselves, because we were moving so fast. We had no idea that Nick was flipping out because he didn't have a clue how to stop the thing."

I remembered the storm and the dead cow spinning down the river when Anna and I went swimming. "How *did* he stop it?"

"We got stuck on a piling under the train trestle." For the first time, Michael looked at me. "They were already searching for us. MacPherson and Armstrong saw us and pulled us out."

"You should have seen Nick's face. He was as gray as the metal on this go-cart." Scott laughed again. "You know something? Nick was the reason I picked up a hammer to really build something for the first time. I wanted to be like him. I wanted to make anything like he could. He could build the coolest stuff."

"He was going to be an engineer," Michael said. "He was going to race cars. He was working on his pilot's license and he was going to build his own airplane. He was going to fly back to Agatha and pick me up in it and take me to the Indianapolis 500 when he raced in it." Michael looked at the racetrack again, like Nick was right there tearing around it.

Anna picked at the grass.

Scott got up. He began to inspect the go-cart more closely.

"Get up for a minute."

Michael got out of the go-cart with a bit of effort. Like he had been sitting in the same position for a very long time. Scott flipped it over on its side. He picked a few tools from the tool box.

"We've still got an hour of sunlight to work on it. Why don't you get the grease and rags we left in the garage."

Michael shrugged a bit and went to search the garage.

We stayed to watch them work on the go-cart until they dragged it out onto the racetrack.

"Come on," said Anna. "He's going to be okay. Let's leave them alone."

I made Michael stop just long enough to let me hug him before Anna and I headed back into Agatha. And as soon as I got back, I phoned Mrs. Bell to let her know Michael was okay.

TEN

Two days later, Uncle Colin injured his arm while he was delivering a foal at Armstrong's Stables.

"It sounds like the baby's head is in the wrong position," Aunt Sandy told me as we stood around in our housecoats just after Mr. Armstrong called early in the morning. "He's going to have to try and turn it so it's coming out the right way."

I threw some fruit and muffins in a bag, while she searched for Uncle Colin's farm kit. With his shirt tail flying, Uncle Colin headed out the door.

During the birth, he not only struggled to keep the mare standing, but with his arm inside her, he also fought to tilt the foal's nose up. His arm was crushed by one of the mare's powerful contractions when she shifted and he slipped against the stable wall. Despite this, with Mr. Armstrong's help he had followed the delivery through to make certain the foal was born alive.

Mr. Armstrong dropped Uncle Colin off at the clinic just before noon. By that time, he was sweating heavily, his face was strained and his skin was gray. He thought he might have a broken bone. He blamed himself for losing his balance and not getting out of the way fast enough. My stomach flipped and my knees went weak when I saw his blue and swollen arm.

Aunt Sandy took one look at it and at Uncle Colin's fading complexion.

"Rachel," she practically shouted as she raced around looking for I wasn't quite sure what, "I've got to get Colin to the hospital. I need you to cancel our appointments for the rest of the day."

She asked me because the receptionist was sick, the veterinary assistant was on holidays and Anna had gone to visit her grandmother in Calgary for the day. Not that I minded in the least.

"Don't worry," I said, handing her the set of keys, which I guessed was what she was looking for — they were sitting smack in the middle of her desk. "I can handle it."

"I know you can." She took the keys. "Okay, Colin. Let's go."

Uncle Colin managed a wilted smile. "You're sure you'll be all right by yourself?"

I felt so bad for him. "Yes, I'll be just fine." I hugged him gently and turned him toward the door. "Now, get going, because you may end up taking me with you if I have to keep looking at that swollen arm."

■ ■ ■

So that is how I ended up in charge of the clinic. All I needed to do was feed the animals and re-schedule the appointments and let's face it, how challenging could either of those things be? I sat at the desk in the room behind the reception area where I could keep an eye on the animals, and I made the phone calls. It took quite a while because almost everyone had questions; they were truly concerned about Uncle Colin and not the least bit upset about losing their appointment for the day.

The one person I couldn't get hold of was Mrs. Currie, who was scheduled to bring in her terrier-poodle cross, Sophie. She was Aunt Sandy's next appointment and she was probably already on her way.

Once the phone calls were made, I turned to feeding the animals. There were only two dogs in the clinic that day: Lady, a setter, who'd broken her leg after falling through a rotten floor board in Shainberg's barn; and Rasmussen's dog Grizzly Bear, a cross between a Doberman and a chow. Grizzly Bear had needed twenty stitches after tangling with a barbed wire fence.

Lady was a sweet, friendly dog, who nearly knocked me over in her enthusiasm to get at her dinner, despite her broken leg. Grizzly Bear, on the other hand, I was not so sure about. I stood before his cage, holding his bowl of food. Up until then, he had just sat there with his brown eyes following every move I made. And when I thought about it, I had never seen him wag his tail and he had never barked, although being so big and black and fiendish looking — if he did make a noise — I knew *exactly* how it would sound. Like the haunting howl of the Hound of the Baskervilles. Like the ghostly death rattle somewhere off in the mist, starting low, climbing higher and higher until it was a heart-stopping, blood-curdling wolf's scream!

"Hi, Rach."

"Aak!" I whirled around. "Michael, you nearly scared me to death!"

"What — by walking through the door? Geez, what are you so jumpy about?"

"I —" I dropped my arm and moved away from Grizzly Bear's kennel.

Michael glanced at him. "Grizzly Bear? Grizzly Bear is scaring you? Grizzly Bear is nothing but a great big baby." Cramming his arm between the bars, he rubbed Grizzly Bear on the nose.

Encouraged by Michael, I went back to where he stood next to Grizzly Bear's kennel.

"Hi, Grizzly Bear," I ventured.

Grizzly Bear cocked his head in a very cute way. He whimpered a little.

"Good boy," I said with a little more confidence. "I guess you're hungry." I opened the kennel door and when I walked in, Grizzly Bear started whipping his tail back and forth like he'd never been so happy to see anyone in his whole life.

"See," Michael said. "You wouldn't be smiling either

if you had to sit in a kennel all by yourself with nothing to do."

I patted Grizzly Bear and left him his food.

For nearly a week, I hadn't seen much of Michael in the afternoons. He and Scott had been spending most of their time out at Abbott's working on Nick's go-cart. When he'd taken me out to see it the night before, I could hardly believe what they'd done. They'd sanded off the rusty spots and put on fancy wheels. They'd got hold of a leather-covered steering wheel and painted the engine silver. They'd done stuff to the engine so it didn't putter like an old sewing machine anymore but roared like an outboard motor.

"How's it going?" I asked, kissing him after rubbing grease off his cheek. I didn't tell him he smelled like a gas pump.

"Great. Wait until you see our paint job. It's red-and-black checkerboard. We're almost done, but Scott wanted to take a break for an hour so I came to see if you wanted to get something to eat at Dot's."

"Michael, I can't. I'm the only one here." And I told him about Uncle Colin delivering the foal.

"Oh man, I hope he's all right. Okay, you stay here and I'll bring you something. Do you want anything in particular or should I surprise you?"

"Isn't it always a surprise with Dot?"

He grinned. "I guess you're right. Okay, I'll be back in fifteen. Don't go anywhere."

The only place I was going was back into Grizzly

Bear's kennel to change his water. I was just closing his door again when Mrs. Currie, moving briskly, marched in the door. At least I assumed it was Mrs. Currie because there was a little terri-poo face peeking out from under one of her arms.

"Hi," I said.

But she didn't say hi back; she just raised her hand in the air, signaling for me to be quiet while her eyes darted quickly around the room. After discovering there was no one to talk to but me, I guess she decided that I would have to do. She waved me over. Her lipstick was extreme and her make-up was thick, packed in the lines of her forehead. Every hair on her silver head was in place. She asked to see Aunt Sandy. Actually, she demanded to see Aunt Sandy.

"I'm sorry," I told her. "I couldn't get hold of you." And once again I explained what had happened with Uncle Colin and his arm. I brought the appointment book out from behind the counter. "I'll have to re-book your appointment for tomorrow."

But when I looked up, Mrs. Currie was frowning. She started giving orders with her hand again. She waved the appointment book aside.

"Forget that. Just tell me when she's going to be back."

"I'm sorry, but I can't tell you exactly when." I wasn't all that sure I liked her attitude. "They had to drive to the hospital in Medicine Hat, so probably not until late this afternoon."

"Well, what does that mean? Four o'clock? Five? Can't you be more specific?"

It was becoming clear that Mrs. Currie had not done her hair and patted on make-up to be turned away. I backed up a bit, and to avoid her eyes, I pretended to study the appointment book.

"Look, I can squeeze you in right here, first thing in the morning."

She lifted her nose in the air. "First thing tomorrow morning."

"Yes, first thing."

"First thing tomorrow morning is not soon enough!"

My mistake was to back up, closer to the wall. But the truth was, I needed the support. I have very little backbone when it comes to people yelling in my face.

"My dear," Mrs. Currie drawled like she had suddenly decided she was talking to someone with limited intelligence, "Sophie has a cough and she can't wait until tomorrow. She needs to see Dr. Hefferman today!"

I didn't get what she wanted me to do! She was staring at me with her nasty little green eyes when, thank God, the telephone rang. She paced impatiently back and forth while I told Mr. Black that he'd have to wait until tomorrow for his cat's prescription. Mr. Black was *soo* nice and understanding; I would have listened to an entire inventory of his hardware store, just to keep from hanging up the phone.

"I want you to call the hospital and find out when

they're going to be back," Mrs. Currie had decided once I hung up.

She had to be kidding. What could Aunt Sandy possibly do from there? Besides, wasn't that a little insensitive?

"Why?" I asked.

It was only one small word, but it was the absolute wrong one because, as I discovered too late, Mrs. Currie was one of those people who did *not* like to hear a question in response to a command. The next thing she did was set Sophie on the floor. She stood across from me. Her many rings clunked against the counter.

"Why? Because I asked you to!" She then leaned so far forward that she was speaking in my face. I plastered myself against the wall. "You know something? *You* are a very insolent young lady. And I think the doctors will be very disappointed when they hear how rude you have been!"

I was *not* insolent, I was *not* being rude, and Mrs. Currie was a mean, self-centered, makeup-smeared hag! Although it didn't help to know this because she still made me feel miserable and incompetent. And as hard as I tried, as much as I knew Uncle Colin would stand up for me, I couldn't stop my chin from trembling.

I didn't hear the door open.

"Hello, Gretchen."

Staring through watery eyes, I looked past Mrs. Currie. Only one person I knew in Agatha had hair like the man now standing inside the door. Rib Bone Squire.

I would never have thought I'd be so happy to see *him*. He was holding the birdhouse I'd seen him sanding outside his cabin, and although his voice was as thin and frail as he looked, Mrs. Currie backed away from the counter when she heard it. Scooping Sophie from the floor, she marched past Rib Bone.

"Richard," she said, nodding curtly. She left the clinic.

Rib Bone came over to where I still cringed against the wall. He set the birdhouse on the counter and after pulling a tissue from the box on the counter, he pressed it into my hand.

"Was Mrs. Currie giving you a hard time?"

I took the tissue. "You could say that."

Grizzly Bear was whining behind me, excited by the sound of his voice.

"Don't take it personally. Rumor has it that she's really a witch. All that make-up? It's just a poor disguise."

I looked at him and smiled. Rib Bone was quite funny. Especially for a murderer.

He nodded toward the kennels. "Although it does make you wonder why a nice dog like Grizzly Bear has to sit in there while Mrs. Currie gets to walk around. Snapping and snarling at people."

I laughed again. "You're right about that."

"Well, it doesn't look like she left too many tooth marks. Is Dr. Bennett not in?"

Feeling much more in control, I told him he wasn't

and what had happened. Rib Bone was very concerned. He patted the roof of the birdhouse on the counter.

"Would you do me a favor and pass this on to him? Along with my wishes that he get better, of course. You can tell him it's from Richard Squire. He'll know what it's for."

"Yes, I will."

"Thank you." But before he left, Rib Bone walked over to Grizzly Bear's kennel where he bent down and, speaking quietly to him, scratched him behind the ears to calm him down.

"Now, you're sure you're all right?" he asked me again on his way out.

I nodded my head.

As soon as the front door closed, I scrambled to watch after him as he walked slowly down the street. Michael was walking down the same sidewalk toward me, carrying a large paper bag. They nodded at one another as they passed.

And oh! — how I wished that Anna had been there.

ELEVEN

The Agatha Rodeo and Exhibition was in a week. Red
and yellow tents blossomed in the open field behind
the grandstand as city workers strung guy lines and
pounded pegs into the hard earth. Mr. Potter put the
finishing touches on the pavilion, trimming the windows and doors in black. Simon helped his dad set up
a barbecue about half a block long. Even Uncle Colin,
despite his broken arm, spent the weekend organizing
the children's petting zoo, because by Thursday afternoon the long trucks carrying pieces and limbs of
midway rides would be rumbling into town.

On Wednesday, Scott and Michael took an afternoon off go-carting to build the game booths. While
they unloaded the table saw from the truck with Mr.
Goodwyn's help, Anna and I rode our bikes around,
pitching in where we were asked.

Mr. Ferguson waved Anna over to grab an end with

Simon while they moved the barbecue nearer to the pavilion. I spread straw over the floor of the petting zoo. Once Scott was set up, he called me over to hold a board steady while he put in some screws. Setting his drill aside, he rummaged in the tool belt around his waist in search of something.

He gave up. "I must have left my bits out at the track."

"Your bits?"

"The bits for my drill. I need them to set in the screws. I forgot them in the tool box in the garage."

"Oh."

Anna was back, standing beside me.

"We'll get them," I told him, letting my end of the board down. Michael was cutting another two-by-four and I had to shout to be heard above the wheeze and scream of the saw. "What do they look like?"

Scott also shouted as he described the case the bits were in. He told us that he really appreciated us going all that way to get them.

"Hey, not a big deal. Saw a board or pound a nail or something," said Anna. "We'll be back in thirty minutes."

We hopped on our bikes and rode off.

I was getting to like Aunt Sandy's bike now that I'd broken it in. It had only taken a new set of tires, a new chain, seat, handle grips and a full can of WD-40, but it ran incredibly smoothly. Although I still had trouble keeping up with Anna on the hills. We raced down the hill into town and back up Rundle Road to the highway. By that time, she was far ahead of me.

"Slow down," I called after her.

She did slow down until I was able to catch up. She picked up speed again. Minutes later I was cruising right behind her across the flat surface when she stopped so suddenly that I rammed into her.

"Anna!"

"That was Megan Gillis that just drove by."

"Yeah, so?"

"Megan Gillis with her mom."

I knew that. I mean, I didn't know that was Megan Gillis that drove by at that moment, but I knew she was back in Agatha and so did Anna. She *had* run away to Calgary to stay with her dad. I wasn't quite sure why Anna was so surprised to see her.

"You knew she was back, Anna. What's the big deal?"

Anna only shook her head. "Nothing, I guess. Never mind."

All right. I would never mind. She rode behind me the last half mile to the track.

The drill bits were exactly where Scott had said they would be. I tucked them in my shorts while Anna straightened the shoddy old tarp covering the go-cart. Not that anyone ever went out there, but if they did, Scott and Michael wanted the go-cart to blend right in with the junk. We closed the door of the garage as best we could, considering there was no doorknob and the door no longer fit the frame. We walked toward our bikes, which we had left leaning against the bleachers. Taylor and Cory were standing beside them. The limousine was parked on the road behind.

"What are you doing here?" Anna demanded.

She said it like she'd found them standing in the middle of her bedroom, which probably wasn't a good way to react because Cory and Taylor seemed to be just driving around. I don't think, at that moment, they had an ulterior motive for being at the track, but Anna's question got them interested in why *we* would be there.

Cory frowned. "We might ask you the same thing. We saw you heading out on the highway when we were filling up at the Shell station."

Anna got a bit defensive when she realized her mistake. "We, um, we just came out to look around. Rachel hasn't been out here yet."

"And are you impressed?"

"Impressed? Oh, yeah." I made a motion toward the saggy bleachers and the dilapidated concession stand. I swept in the sunken garage. "It looks like it might have been fun. You know, at one time." I didn't like the suspicious way Cory was looking at me. "A long time ago."

"Hey, Cory!" We all turned toward Taylor, who was standing in the center of the racetrack, swiping at the dirt with his foot. "Look at this. Someone's been out here. With wheels. These are fresh tire tracks."

I had to be impressed. It really was an amazingly keen observation for Taylor. But — it also meant that we were pretty much dead.

Cory glanced curiously from Anna to me before he went over to check out the tire tracks for himself. He walked back over to us.

"Where's the go-cart?"

"I don't know what you're talking about." I backed toward the bicycles, tripped on an old tire and fell on my butt.

Anna didn't move.

"Anna," I whispered, smacking dust from my hands, "let's get back. Scott needs his drill bits."

It turned out to be just about the stupidest thing I could have said.

"Drill bits?" Cory lifted an eyebrow. "Why would Cardinal need tools out here?"

"I, uh, who said he needed tools out here?"

Cory and Taylor both headed for the garage. We ran after them. It took them all of thirty seconds to find Nick's go-cart. They threw the moldy tarp aside. They pushed the go-cart out of the garage and onto the racetrack, ignoring Anna and me as we hopped along beside it. We told them it was Nick's go-cart and that they had better not touch it. That Scott and Michael had worked their butts off to get it running and look-ing the way it did, and that if anything happened to it, Michael would kill them.

"You know what?" said Taylor. "We don't care."

Cory started it up. They laughed at the kick and roar of the engine.

"Power!" bellowed Taylor. "Cardinal didn't hold back!"

Cory revved it a few more times, got comfortable in the seat and took off around the racetrack. We stood on the side, screeching and yelling and begging him to stop and put the go-cart back in the garage. If they did it now, we tried to convince them, Michael and Scott would never know. Cory only reacted by swerving, threatening to mow us down, mulch us into the prairie dust. We leapt back, straight into a bed of thistles.

"You jerk!" Anna shrieked, shaking a fist. But we bore the thistles and bits of flying gravel sprayed at us as if we deserved them. It was all our fault.

"I should have acted naturally," Anna moaned. "Like it was no big thing them being here."

"I shouldn't have said anything about the tools."

Taylor stood on the side of the track making stupid car noises and shifting imaginary gears. He signaled for Cory to pull over and let him take a turn driving.

I jangled the metal drill bits in my pocket. This was not going to be good. I knew how Taylor drove a car. And I was right. Taylor tore around the track like he was trying to get airborne. We yelled at him to slow down. Even Cory shouted something when Taylor ripped around a corner on two wheels.

"Let's go," I said, bolting toward our bikes. "They're not going to listen to us. We've got to get Michael and Scott."

Anna followed me toward the bleachers.

"Taylor!" Cory bellowed.

We skidded to a stop.

I guess we'd known right from the beginning that Taylor would crack it up. It's funny how predictable some things are. It happened right in front of us, just after Cory's warning, when Taylor was up on two wheels. Strained beyond its limits, a front wheel flew off and soared across the fence into the next field. The go-cart went down on its axle. Sparks flew from the metal as it tore across the gravel. Taylor lost what little control he had and careened into the bleachers. We jumped back as the benches collapsed and fell. Speechless, we watched helplessly as the last boards toppled into each other in a great cloud of dust.

We rushed over to the go-cart and stared at it in horror. All of Scott and Michael's work — all of Nick's go-cart — was demolished. Cory jogged over and stood beside us. Taylor struggled out of the crumpled metal heap. He had a small blue bump on his forehead and his hand was bleeding. Nobody said anything right away.

"Well? Isn't anyone going to ask if I'm all right?"

"You moron!" Anna answered, belting him across the arm.

Cory walked around the go-cart while Anna and I continued to gape at it, wishing there was some way to turn back time.

"Hey! I'm bleeding here." Taylor touched two fingers to the bump on his head.

"Know what?" Anna seethed. "We don't care."

Cory pulled the leather steering wheel off the rod and tossed it in the air. It spun across the track like a drunken Frisbee, skidding to a stop against the garage.

"Hey! It wasn't my fault. If the thing had been built right, it wouldn't have happened. Tell Cardinal *that*, Anna."

"I've got a better idea. *You* tell him. And while you're at it, why don't you explain to Michael why you smashed up Nick's go-cart?!"

That shut Taylor up for several seconds because, with the mention of Nick, I think it suddenly struck him what he had done. Taylor could be a real twit and a thug, but when it came right down to it, he wasn't a total psychopath. He mumbled something, kicked the one intact wheel on the go-cart and walked toward his limousine. Cory followed him. We could hear them arguing from where we paced on the grass.

We considered how we were going to tell Michael. After much discussion we decided not to tell him. We would get Scott alone and tell him instead.

Cory and Taylor returned to the smashed-up go-cart. They didn't tell us what they were planning, but it was apparent they had something in mind.

"What are you going to do?" Anna skipped beside them as they freed the go-cart from the bleachers. We both followed them as they dragged it into the garage. Cory picked up a can of gasoline and sloshed it all over the rags. He slopped it over the cardboard boxes stacked against the walls. He splashed it all over the ground.

He pulled his lighter from his pocket. With the first snap, a soft blue flame jumped up.

"Don't you dare," Anna warned him.

"Shut up, Anna. And get out." He picked up a rag and lit it.

"Don't be an idiot, Cory. You're only making it worse."

"It's an old building. Look around you. It's full of oily rags and gasoline and all kinds of hazardous stuff. This way, it's just gone."

"Cory! Scott and Michael are not stupid. It doesn't matter what you do; they're still going to find out."

Which we suspected was the reason Cory and Taylor were going to the trouble that they were to destroy what Taylor had done. This was serious stuff and there was no way Scott, and especially Michael, would let it slide. Not this time. They knew that.

"Get out."

"What makes you think *we* won't tell them?"

"Because it would be very bad for your health if you do. If it's an accident, they'll just accept it. You won't have to listen to them freak out and we won't have to break any of your bones."

Grabbing both Anna and me by the arms, Taylor yanked us into the yard, well away from the garage.

"Cory!"

Cory threw the burning rag and leapt back from where he stood by the open garage doors. With a loud woosh, flames shot across the floor. They consumed the cardboard boxes, swept up the walls and touched off the split dry wood. Then there was the hot sun. And an encouraging breeze. Once the walls were engulfed in flames, it was only a matter of minutes before the old garage fell.

We heard several small explosions. The heat was searing and we moved back to avoid melting. Bits of floating ash flew past our faces and we were soon choking on the ugly smell of burning rubber as heavy black smoke clouds rolled up and away into the sky.

Cory and Taylor returned to the limousine and drove away.

Anna and I wanted to go for help, but we were afraid to leave. We'd already stamped out several small fires that had jumped from the burning building to the dry grass. We could only hope that someone would soon see the smoke.

By the time Michael and Scott drove up in Mr. Goodwyn's truck, the building was not much more than smoking embers and the metal had all turned black.

"Jeezus, what happened?" Michael demanded, tearing up next to us.

"Holy *shit*!" Scott spouted in disbelief.

They both stared at the flagging fire and then at us, waiting for an answer. Anna looked to me for support. She told them what Taylor and Cory had done.

When she was finished, Michael picked up the leather steering wheel from the grass where it had bounced after Cory threw it against the garage.

"Those pricks! I'll kill them!" He hurled it into the fire. "The engine alone took us two full days!" He picked up a wheel and hurled that in too. "We had to get the sprockets specially machined!"

And before they took off after Cory and Taylor, we'd heard how they'd searched all over town to find the perfect wheels, and how they'd talked Mr. Armstrong into giving them the steering wheel off the ancient BMW that was parked inside his barn.

Michael tore up the earth as he drove off in the truck.

"Know something?" Anna said as we watched after them. "He didn't even mention Nick."

I looked at her. No, he hadn't mentioned Nick. But Nick had been there all right – he'd been behind every word that Michael had spit out.

TWELVE

At two o'clock in the morning I heard Michael calling my name. At first I thought it was in a dream, but I kept hearing it, anxious and whispered. I sat up. It was coming through the window. I pulled the blind aside.

"Michael."

In the flat light of the street lamp he looked terrible; his face was drained and he still wore the same clothes he'd been sawing boards in earlier that day.

"I need to talk to you," he said.

I opened the window wide to let him in.

"What is it? What's wrong? Where have you been?"

"We couldn't find them." He crawled through the window and dropped to the floor. Pacing back and forth, he spoke in a low whisper. "They knew we'd be after them. They're hiding. They took off and we've looked everywhere. We even drove out to Cypress Hills."

He was really wired. His words were clipped and

his hands moved crazily as he spoke. I took his hand and pulled him down next to me to sit on the edge of the bed.

"Where's Scott?"

"He went home. He gives up too easily. I guess they could have driven down to Lethbridge, but I don't know why, and anyway, they would have been back by now." His leg wouldn't stop jiggling. I tried to calm him down by laying my hand across his knee.

"Michael, maybe that's not such a bad idea."

"What?"

"What Scott did. Maybe you should go home too."

"Huh?" He looked at me like I was nuts. Like that wasn't even a consideration.

"Just for tonight," I quickly added. "You can deal with it in the morning."

He jumped to his feet, whispering, "No!"

Obviously, it was not what he had come to hear.

"Okay, okay." And I didn't say anything else, because I had no idea what he wanted me to say.

As he continued to pace back and forth, I was thankful the house was silent. Uncle Colin and Aunt Sandy had gone to bed just before midnight after watching a movie. They'd invited Anna and me to watch it with them, but between our unanswered phone calls to Michael's and to Scott's, we'd spent the evening in my room, discussing whether or not to tell Uncle Colin about the fire. We wanted to tell him because this thing between Scott and Michael, and Cory and Taylor was getting out of hand. We were afraid to tell him because of how Scott — well, mostly how Michael would react. We also didn't want to tell him because Cory and Taylor would kill us.

Michael sat next to me on the bed again.

"Look, I'm sorry," he said, pulling me close to him. When he rested his head on my shoulder, I could feel his heart racing against my chest. I brought my arms around his shoulders. It surprised me to find his muscles so tight.

"Rach, you don't get it. That guy has been a thorn in my side since I was a kid. I just can't let this go."

I knew that wasn't the real reason, but I wasn't going to say anything, not considering the state he was in. And then I thought I heard a noise.

"Michael, this is not a good idea. I'm not telling you to drop it entirely. Only for tonight. Go home. Please? I'll call you first thing in the morning."

It was so hard to look at the rejection on his face, and I realize now that he had come to me because I was the last comfort he could cling to. Although I didn't know it then, I had just destroyed that,

He dropped his arms from around me. His leg stopped vibrating and he stood up to leave.

"All right," he said. There was a change in his voice, like he'd arrived at some kind of a decision, and I thought that maybe he was agreeing that going home was the right thing to do.

"Michael?"

Hiking himself up onto the windowsill, he swung his legs out into the night.

"When will I see you?"

He didn't answer me. He hit the ground and walked across the lawn to the road.

■ ■ ■

I called Michael at ten o'clock that morning. He was in the shower, so I left a message with his mom that Scott, Anna and I would meet him in Dot's Diner at noon. Scott was already working on the game booths. Anna and I wandered up to the exhibition grounds to see if there was anything we could do. As we tromped up the hill, two trucks hauling chuckwagons chugged past us, and then — a cattle truck thundered by. A sudden squall of foul air rushed past me and I held my breath until my lungs nearly burst. *Phew*! If I could hardly breathe for those few seconds, it made me wonder how the poor animals packed inside ever managed to survive.

Scott didn't need our help. Not unless we knew how to operate a table saw or an electric nail gun, and, of course, neither Anna or I qualified for either one. He was nearly finished anyway, so to pass time we walked past the stables with their new sweaty smell of horses and out along the railroad tracks. I picked up a withered old cow pie and hucked it to the other side of the fence, where it exploded into a puff of dust. I told Anna about Michael coming to the house during the night.

"Anna, I'm getting worried. He was in pretty rough shape."

She had been listening quietly to what I was telling her. "Yeah, well, I told you he gets like that sometimes. Give him a few days. He'll calm down." I knew she was trying to sound reassuring, but I could tell that even she wasn't convinced of her own words.

We traipsed along, thinking and talking about the fire and wondering where all this might go. After a while I stopped and looked up at the horizon. Camped above the sprawling plain was a hard gray sky. It had been like that, off and on, between bursts of sunshine for the past several days; threatening another torrential downpour, but not raining. We decided to turn around.

"Rachel!" Anna hissed in my ear. She froze with her fingers clamped onto my bare arm.

Rib Bone Squire, bent and dependent on his walking stick, was coming toward us. He was following the railroad tracks on his way back from town.

"I see him," I said.

"What's he doing coming back so early?" Anna's fingernails bit into me.

I shook her. "Anna, you're going to walk right by him and you're going to act natural."

"Impossible. Let's turn around and run!"

"No. That would be extremely rude." I started walking again, dragging Anna along behind me like I was hauling a washing machine. "I told you he's a really good guy. All you need to do is smile nicely and say hi."

By that point we were within hearing distance of Rib Bone, so Anna didn't say anything more. Rib Bone moved closer. We moved closer. With each step, he settled the tip of his walking stick against a tie. I pulled Anna off the tracks and onto the grass to give him a wider berth. He was concentrating on his feet and I don't think he even noticed us coming until we were ten feet in front of him. That's when Anna took a step in his direction and practically shouted, "Hi!"

Surprised, Rib Bone missed his target. The walking stick sank into the soft gravel and he lost his balance. But he didn't fall, because Anna flew across the tracks and caught him by the arm. She supported him until he was standing on two sure feet again. He slapped a hand to his chest.

"Thank you, young lady. My, you almost gave an old man a heart attack. Hasn't anyone ever told you it's not a good idea to creep up on old people like that?" He was talking to Anna but he winked at me. And then – Rib Bone smiled. And when he did, his eyes lit up and his face folded in a thousand different places.

I wasn't sure if it was his joke or the cartoon look of his face or the discovery that Rib Bone Squire was not a monster, but Anna smiled back. She held his arm a little longer.

"Well," he waggled his stick at the big gray sky. "You girls had better get to wherever you're going. Another hour and that sky's going to open up."

Anna didn't budge. "Do you think so?"

It was really weird. It was like she *wanted* to talk to him now.

"I mean, it's been like that for the past two days."

"Yes, it has. But the wind has stopped." He swept his cane through the air. "And so have the meadowlarks. Listen." He held a hand to his ear.

And so – we listened. Anna and I stood there with Rib Bone Squire and we listened. We stood there, three little specks beneath the heavy gray sky; three small regular people in the middle of the flat yellow prairie with the whole universe above us. In the field beside us the cattle stood huddled together, but other than the odd low moo, there was not a sound. Certainly not the distinct trill of the meadowlark.

"I don't hear them," said Anna.

"That's because they know there's a storm coming. They've already taken shelter and I suggest that you two do the same." With that, Rib Bone gave a small salute with his cane and started down the railroad track again. "Oh," remembering something, he turned around. "That cave – and the storms we've been having – it's unstable. You kids should stay away from there."

So, all summer long, as we'd huddled in the cave and Anna had told stories of the monstrous things he'd done, he'd known that we were there.

"Yes," I told him. I poked Anna. "We will."

Rib Bone continued down the track. Anna looked after him and for some time she didn't say a thing. She only stared after Rib Bone's small crumpled figure.

"Mr. Squire!" she suddenly shouted.

Rib Bone turned around.

"I'm real sorry about your dog. Watson? I'm real sorry."

Rib Bone nodded, waved his cane once again and was on his way.

Anna watched him go.

"Come on," I said, tugging her sleeve. "Let's see if Scott is done." I started jogging, but she snapped me to a halt by grabbing hold of my waistband. When I turned around, she had this amazed look on her face. "What is it?"

"Rachel, Rib Bone's not such a bad guy."

She was *so* stating the obvious that I laughed. "No, he's not. I told you that. Now let's go."

Still, she didn't move. "And he didn't kill Megan Gillis."

"Yeah, well, no duh. But you've known that for a week." I was getting a little impatient. "What's this sudden revelation?"

"No, see, he's never killed anybody. He's never done anything criminal as long as I've been alive."

"Anna, isn't that what I've been telling you? Isn't that what Scott and Michael have always told you? So now you believe them?"

"And he didn't kill Lucy MacPherson. I think it was all a bunch of hype and I believed the stories. That's what really *bugs* me."

"Anna, it wasn't just you. Lots of people believed those stories."

"Yeah, they believed them for the same reason I did. Because somebody told them and they didn't even bother to check them out. But if they thought about it, like I have, they would figure it out. Look at the old guy — what's he ever done? He walks into town a couple of times a week. He goes about his business and he doesn't bother anybody. And he really loved his dog." Anna stared at me like she was accusing me of something.

"Anna," I turned my palms in the air, "I'm with you."

She flew ahead of me down the railroad tracks toward the exhibition grounds, and for a moment, I stood there watching her. And I couldn't help thinking how in a small way she had been like one of those poor animals jammed in the cattle truck, and someone had stopped in the middle of a big green field, opened a door and let her free.

■　■　■

It was unusual to see Scott uptight as we sat in Dot's Diner, waiting for Michael, just before noon. I hadn't seen him get uptight about anything all summer, but then, I suppose we were all a bit uptight. We weren't quite sure how far Michael would want to take this go-cart thing. So we were a little relieved when he strode up to our table with his hands stuffed in his pockets, looking — well, tired more than anything. He smiled as he shot a box across the table toward Scott.

Scott's face brightened. "Hey, it came."

Michael slid next to me in the booth. "Yeah, this morning."

"What is it?" Anna and I asked.

"The collector's edition of *Army of Darkness*. I ordered it over the net."

Picking at the french fries she and Scott were sharing, Anna groaned. Scott eagerly scanned the blurb on the back of the box. Michael asked if I had ordered anything to eat.

"No," I said, "I was waiting for you."

Michael really wasn't hungry, so when Dot came over to our table, we just ordered Cokes and nachos. Once Dot had left, I glanced around the room. We were the only people in the diner aside from Mrs. MacPherson and Bradley, who was trying to catch Michael's attention. I pointed him out. Michael smiled and returned a big wave. He hadn't mentioned the go-cart or the fire, and I sure wasn't going to be the first to bring it up.

Scott handed the movie back to Michael. "Let's watch it this afternoon."

Michael seemed strangely hesitant, but he agreed. He tried to convince Anna and me to watch it with them. Anna flatly refused. She did not want to watch one of their brain-dead, stupidly violent horror movies. I raised my eyebrows. Put that way, I was with her.

Michael didn't give up. "Come on, Rach. It's not the least bit scary. It's funny."

"A *funny* horror movie? I didn't know there was such a thing."

"Yeah, the army is just a bunch of skeletons that rise from their graves. You'll laugh," he told me, although he wasn't smiling. Mostly, I realized, because what he was saying was really not what was on his mind.

Dot arrived with our drinks. It was when Michael pushed mine down the table toward me that I first noticed the blood-soaked bandage covering his hand.

I pulled in my breath. "Michael, what did you do to your hand?!"

He left the glass on the table in front of me, made a fist of his hand and parked it in his lap. He attempted to brush the whole thing aside.

"I cut myself working. Yesterday. It was just stupid."

I reached over. Reluctantly, he let me take his hand in mine. I carefully pried his fingers open. I was really shocked, because judging by the amount of blood that had soaked through the pink elastic bandage, it was much deeper than a simple cut.

"You did this yesterday and it's still bleeding like this? Don't you think you should get stitches?!"

He pulled his hand back. "No."

Anna bent over the table. "Let me see that."

"No."

I couldn't believe he was just sitting there, drinking a Coke, bleeding to death.

"I don't need stitches. I've cut myself dozens of times."

Dot came back to the table carrying a basket of nachos. Scott was looking curiously at Michael as she asked if we needed anything else. Michael seemed to have trouble meeting his eyes. I told Dot no, thank you, we didn't need anything else. Once she had left, Michael pushed the basket aside.

"I don't even feel like this. I should go out to Goodwyn's farm." He stood up. "I've got a bunch of work to do."

"You said you'd watch the movie," Scott reminded him, also getting up from the booth. His tone was almost insistent.

Michael thought for a moment.

"Yeah, all right," he finally agreed.

■ ■ ■

After they left, Anna and I walked down to the clinic. Uncle Colin was not expecting us, but he was very glad to see us. No one else was around and Lucifer, a scrappy Siamese cat, was giving him a hard time. He was trying to change the dressing around Lucifer's neck, but his broken arm was only getting in the way. So while I held the cat tightly against my chest, Anna held his back legs together so he wouldn't kick. Lucifer let out a marathon howl like he was being forced to endure the worst kind of torture. We all laughed.

Uncle Colin peeled off the dressing covering the wound.

"Did your friends find you?" he asked me.

"What friends?"

"Cory Sparks and the Sparshatts' boy, Taylor."

Anna's eyes darted to mine.

"No."

"Hold this for a sec, will you, Rachel?" I held the end of the new tape taut while he snipped it. "Anyway, they were in here about an hour ago. Apparently Taylor's car was stolen last night. He's probably telling everyone he knows in case they hear anything. There, Lucifer, all done. Now was that really so bad?"

THIRTEEN

Taylor's limousine was discovered at the bottom of Sullivan's Pond early the next morning. Mr. Ferguson had closed his restaurant for the day to go fishing, and with his first cast he'd snagged the grisly little skull that hung from the rearview mirror. It must have floated through one of the windows that Michael had smashed.

Scott and Michael, along with everyone else who knew Taylor, were questioned by the police. Yeah, sure they goofed around a bit, but they were still pretty good guys. Constable Rutledge knew they were and he had no reason not to believe them. Late in the afternoon, he told Taylor's dad that he didn't have any solid leads yet. He also didn't have a lot of time. He had been on the trail of a couple of poachers for the past few weeks and he was getting ready to nail them. Still, he would continue questioning the locals and check into the backgrounds of any transients who might have been through town.

Michael was not home when I called his house. Anna and I tried to talk to Scott about what Michael had done, but he didn't seem to want to talk to us. He left for Armstrong's Stables right after his talk with Constable Rutledge. He was anxious to get the fencing done before school started, he told us; he didn't have time to just hang around.

I didn't see Michael again until I was walking home after watching a movie at Sylvie's house that night. I had left right after it was over, although Anna stayed. I was feeling pretty rotten and I wanted to try phoning Michael one more time.

He was sitting alone on the steps of the train station as I walked by. I was surprised to see him just sitting there in the fading light — especially after I'd spent a good part of the day trying to find him. He was all curled over with his head in his hands and his elbows resting on his knees. He didn't look up until I was almost right by his side.

"Hey, Michael."

"Hey." He glanced up only briefly before returning to the trains again. Which made me think he wasn't incredibly overjoyed to see me. I wasn't going to leave.

"How are you? How's your hand?"

Michael twisted the watch on his wrist.

"It's all right."

I sat on the step beside him.

He kept twisting the watch. It was a beautiful watch

and I hadn't seen him wear it before.

"Can I see that?"

Immediately, he stopped twisting it and dropped his arm to his side so that it was covered by his sleeve.

"Come on, let me see it." I held out my hand. "Please?"

Reluctantly, he pushed back his sleeve and showed me the watch. It was a gorgeous watch, a mechanical watch he told me, and he took it off to show me how you could see the movement through the glass cover on the back, the gears and the flywheel working.

"Wow, this is really cool."

"Yeah, that's why Nick wanted it. He was always into neat stuff like this. Mom joked that at least he wouldn't have to take it apart to see how it worked. Like everything else he had."

"It was Nick's?"

"Yeah, it was Nick's. Although he never saw it. It was his graduation present. He was going to get it the day after his grad party." My eyes followed his finger as it traveled around the gold rim. "Anyway, I've got it now."

It was quiet in the railway yard. There were no screeching brakes or clanging bells or banging cars. Only the tinny jingle of a wind chime dangling from the overhang of the train station.

"It would have been nice if he'd at least seen it though."

"Michael, we haven't talked much about it, but I am so sorry about Nick."

"Yeah, well, so am I." Michael got to his feet. He leaned against the fence, facing me, with his foot resting on the platform of the train station. Above his head there was a great sweep of stars just beginning to bloom in the sky. "You know what's always bugged me, Rach? I mean, what was really lousy about the whole thing?"

I shook my head.

"Nick never got into trouble. He got straight A's in school. He was the captain of his soccer team and he cut old man Butler's grass for nothing. He cut it because Butler was old and he couldn't do it himself. He just never did anything wrong, except when he was younger and he got curious and took things apart because he couldn't help himself. But he didn't drink and he wasn't into anything criminal. And then the one time he slips up — he gets killed. How fair is that?"

"Michael," I said, "it's not fair at all."

"No, it's not." He shoved his hands in his pockets and nervously jangled the change. "Hey, you've got a brother. What's he like?"

"Sean's into his saxophone. He's gone away to college this year."

"Oh, yeah? Miss him?"

I shrugged. "I guess. He hasn't been gone long enough for me to really notice."

"Yeah, well, you will. And so will your parents. I just hope they handle things better than mine." Michael lifted his head and for what I guessed was probably the first time that evening, he noticed the bed of stars.

"Wow, it's dark. I guess I've been here for quite a while. They were welding new track on the spur line when I got here, but it looks like everyone has gone home."

"Uh-huh," I nodded. "Probably about three hours ago." I stood in front of him. "Michael, what do you mean about your mom and dad and handling things?"

At first, I was sorry I'd asked because he instantly looked away. But after a minute he turned back, brought his arm up and began to fidget with Nick's watch again.

"I don't want you to get this wrong," he told me. "I don't want you to think I'm a jerk or anything, I mean, not anymore than you already do. Nick was my brother. He was the greatest and I had a lot of good times with him and it's incredible how much I miss him. I'll never forget him. The thing is, I have to move on or I'm going to crack up. But I can't. My parents won't listen. It's almost like they want to prevent it from happening. In fact, they still spend so much time remembering that Nick is dead, they seem to have forgotten that I'm alive."

I must have looked pretty grim because he laughed a little.

"Oh, forget it. It's hard to explain. Come on Rach, you want me to walk you home?"

"Yeah. But you don't have to. It's out of your way."

"It's not out of my way. Hey — how can you go out of your way when you don't know where you're going?"

I smiled, shrugging off what he said as typical Michael.

We stepped from the platform and began walking down the street. After a while, I took his hand. As we walked, we didn't talk about Taylor's limousine, or us, or any of the stuff that was inside us. It was just too hard to get started and there was just too much to say.

We were passing the high school parking lot when Cory and Taylor rose from the shadows like ghosts. They had been sitting on the bike racks and we hadn't noticed them in the dark as we walked by.

"Bell?"

We turned around. Cory stood on the sidewalk, backed by moonlight. Taylor stepped forward from the dark and stood next to him.

Michael let go of my hand. "What do you want?"

"We're willing to let it go. We'll call it even." Cory raised his palms in the air, signaling a truce. "Your go-cart. Taylor's limo. What do you say?"

I glanced at Taylor. His jaw was set tight and his fists were clenched. This was clearly not the way he wanted to handle it, but he didn't have much choice, not when Michael could pin the fire at Abbott's on them.

Still, I wished that Michael would have been able to go along with it. It might have allowed them to go back to the insults and the practical jokes; the way things had been all their lives. But I guess, inside, I knew that he couldn't. Because what was even to Cory — and what was even to Michael — were now two very different things.

"Forget it." Michael turned his back and started

down the sidewalk.

"Hey!" Taylor called after him. "Shit for brains! Why did you drown my car?! At least what I did was an accident!"

Michael didn't answer.

Taylor couldn't hold back any longer. I screamed when he rushed at Michael. But Michael must have been expecting it because he turned and landed a solid punch in Taylor's stomach. Taylor staggered back a bit, but as angry as he was, he quickly recovered. He swung his fist, cracking Michael across the jaw.

"Michael!" I cried as he slammed into the ground. I bent down next to him, but he pushed me away. Sitting up, he shook his head and wiped blood from his mouth with the back of his hand.

"Just go," I told Taylor. My voice was shaking as I stood up, blocking the space between them.

"But he trashed my car!"

"Just get out of here."

Behind me, Michael was struggling to his feet.

"Cory?" I pleaded.

Finally, Cory pulled Taylor back by his shoulders. "Come on."

Taylor resisted. "I don't get this. Why should he get away with it?"

Cory quietly said something to him.

Taylor slowly backed off. But before he turned and headed in the other direction, he muttered, "Bell's gone completely insane."

They left us alone.

"Are you okay?" I asked. "Look at this, you're still bleeding."

"Yeah, I'm fine," he said, dabbing the corner of his mouth with the tail of his T-shirt. "Come on, let's go." He took my arm and we began walking again. We had walked half a block when he surprised me by laughing a little. "Taylor's not the only one pissed off at me. I'm sure Scott would like to take a swing at me too." But his smile faded as quickly as it came. We didn't say anything else until we were standing in front of Uncle Colin's house.

"When are you leaving?" Michael asked me.

"To go back home?"

He nodded.

"Mom and Dad are coming down from Yellowknife a week from tomorrow. We'll be flying home the next day."

"God," he said, "I'm really going to miss you."

"I'm going to miss you too." His mouth was swollen a little on one side, so I kissed him carefully, then held him to me.

After a while he stood back a bit and looked over my head. "Hey, Rach, why don't you come down to the cave with me?"

"Right now?"

"Yeah, right now. The light is incredible out there; the way the moon bounces off the river and the lights of Agatha glittering off in the distance and the shooting stars — every direction you look there are stars sailing across the sky!"

I smiled, because for one sentence that evening Michael was the enthusiastic guy I had come to know that summer.

"Is it better than a movie?"

"Better than a movie."

"Better than the skeletons rising from their graves in *Army of Darkness*?"

He laughed. "I guess it depends on your mood. When Scott and I used to camp out there, we'd stay awake half the night just watching them."

I really wanted to. In fact, at that moment, it was *all* I wanted to do. I wanted to sit on the edge of the prairie down by Buffalo Coulee with Michael. I wanted to watch the moon skate across the river and the stars fall out of the sky.

"Michael, it's late. I should really go in."

He glanced at Uncle Colin's house.

"Yeah, all right." He started backing down the street. "Well, look after yourself."

I remember thinking at the time that it was an odd thing for him to say. I mean, considering how close we had become and everything. Besides, it wasn't like I was leaving Agatha the next morning.

"Yeah, I will. You too."

Michael waved. He then turned and walked quickly down the street like he knew exactly where he was going.

"See you tomorrow," I called after him.

I saw him lift his hand. And then, even though the night was clear, I felt a raindrop on my cheek. And another.

"Michael, it's starting to rain."

But Michael was already bounding down the street in that way he had.

■ ■ ■

I lay in bed that night listening to the waning voices of the storm. The first furious downpour was over and the rain now pattered softly against the roof. It flowed through the eaves trough. It splashed down the drainpipes and into the big-chested rain barrel Aunt Sandy kept at the side of the house to water the garden. It lifted the scent of wild roses from beneath my window into my room.

Far in the distance I heard the train whistle. A long, sullen cry in the wet night as it rolled across the prairie toward Agatha. It grew louder, and after a while I could feel it rumble into town. As I lay in bed, I felt its great weight as it shuddered across the earth. I heard it brake and slide to a long slow stop in the railway yard.

Minutes later, I heard the spray from Aunt Sandy's tires as she turned down the street and into the driveway. I heard the solid sound of the car door close and her small footsteps splash up to the door. I heard the relief in Uncle Colin's voice when she told him that the mare and the foal he had delivered were much stronger. He needn't worry, they were both going to be just fine.

But there was something I didn't hear that night. Something none of us heard that night. None of us, except Michael. It was the roar of water as it washed through the cave down by Buffalo Coulee. It was the rapid patter of earth falling to the well-tamped floor.

Only Michael breathed the musty smell of wet clay as it swept through the cave and slopped over the edge into Buffalo Coulee.

None of us felt the emptiness that Michael felt. The sense of loss that overwhelmed him as he stood watching another chunk of his life falter, knowing it, too, would soon disappear.

FOURTEEN

I didn't sleep very well that night. I couldn't stop thinking about Michael. I thought about how he used to camp down by Buffalo Coulee with Scott and watch the stars fall from the sky. I thought about how much I had missed who he was in the last week. I wondered how the same person that could be lulled to sleep by the wail of coyotes could do what he had done. I decided it could only be someone who was desperate. Someone who hurt so much inside, they could no longer stand the pain.

Propping myself up on my pillows, I watched the objects in my room come into focus in the early morning light. I remembered how Michael had told me he didn't know where he was going the night before, and how he had bounced down the street after he left me.

I was about to get up when the telephone rang. It was Mrs. Bell. I guess I'd almost been expecting it. She told Uncle Colin that Michael had not come home. Did we have *any* idea where he might be?

I dressed, skipped breakfast and while Uncle Colin glanced up from his newspaper now and again, I paced back and forth across the kitchen floor. I volunteered to ride over and feed the animals at the clinic so he didn't have to rush. When I got back, I read for a while but I couldn't concentrate. Finally, I slipped back into my room and called Anna. I didn't have to convince her of a thing. She had also got the phone call and had already come to the same decision that I had. We had to tell someone about Michael and what he had done. What he might do. Not to be jerks or to save ourselves from anything – but to save Michael from himself.

Half an hour later, Anna came over to the house and we told Uncle Colin about the fire and Taylor's car and the whole crazy mess. When we'd finished, he thanked us. We climbed into his jeep along with Aunt Sandy and we drove over to Michael's house.

That was when we discovered that Scott hadn't really been trying to avoid us. He'd just had a lot on his mind. He'd needed some time to figure it out. It couldn't have been easy to come to the decision that he made: to turn his very best friend in to the police. But, I guess like us, the responsibility of Michael had become too much for him.

Mrs. Bell answered the door. She was crying and Aunt Sandy put an arm around her as we followed her into the living room. We sat down on the dining room chairs Michael's dad set out for us. For the next few minutes, I watched as his parents moved around the room without purpose, like shadows blown in through window. When they finally sat down, Constable Rutledge shuffled his big black boots. His voice boomed into the solemn air.

"All right. Do you kids have any idea where Michael might have gone?"

We looked at each other. Scott suggested Palliser Point Park and Sullivan's Pond. He shrugged. "Or I suppose he could have gone out to Abbott's go-cart track again. Although I guess there's nothing there."

I glanced at him. He hadn't mentioned the cave. My guess was that he wanted one more chance to get to Michael first. I noticed a photograph on the table beside me. Nick, grinning, with one arm hung around Michael. Nick, blond and solid, so unlike Michael physically, but with the same sly smile in his eyes.

"Anybody know what kind of mood he was in? Who saw him last?"

I looked at Mrs. Bell, who was crying quietly, and it struck me how I had never seen anyone so sad.

"Probably me," I said.

The telephone rang. Mrs. Bell flew into the kitchen to answer it. It was Rib Bone Squire. He was anxious to talk to Constable Rutledge. Earlier that morning, someone had broken into his cabin and stolen the shotgun from its cabinet on the wall. Mrs. Bell began to cry uncontrollably. Aunt Sandy sat on the couch next to her, trying to comfort her with soothing words.

Constable Rutledge lay a hand on Mr. Bell's arm. "Okay, David. Colin. Let's go for a drive."

They decided to take Uncle Colin's jeep. We watched through the window as the three men slid into it, and as soon as they were gone, the three of us took off toward the fairgrounds on our bikes.

It was the first real sunny day in a week. It was also the first day of the Agatha Exhibition and Rodeo, which meant there was so much traffic it was an effort just to get up the hill. Near the entrance we hopped off our bikes and elbowed past parents pushing strollers and towing squalling kids with balloons tied to their wrists. Scott nearly knocked over Mr. MacPherson, who clutched a giant panda bear to his chest while Bradley hung on to one of the legs. We hopped on our bikes again.

We rode next to the fence outside the fairgrounds. From a distance we could see Simon flipping hamburgers with a big spatula. He waved a sudden burst of smoke from his eyes. We passed the midway where Cory was ripping tickets and Taylor was strapping kids into the bumper cars.

"I just remembered. I'm supposed to be in the day care wiping runny noses."

"What?"

It was impossible to compete with the loudspeakers and the chuckwagon races and the midway with its pulsing noise.

"Never mind."

Soon we met up with the railroad track. We bumped along beside it as we crossed O'Conner's ranch, leaving the voices of the exhibition behind us.

Anna pulled next to Scott. "Why didn't you tell them about the cave?"

"They'll figure it out. I wanted a chance to get to him first."

"You don't even know if he's there."

"I have a pretty good hunch."

We dropped our bikes where the railroad track curved toward the river.

"Mike!" Scott shouted the instant we dropped them. "Mike!" He hopped the fence and peeled ahead of us down the path.

We stumbled behind him, tripping over new ruts where the heavy rains had cut into the ground. Anna fell on her knees and I nearly ended up tumbling the rest of the way down the hill.

"Mike!" Scott stood in the entrance to the cave, blocking it. And he kept on standing there. He didn't go in and he didn't say anything more. Not for many seconds. Finally, he murmured, "Oh, man, what have you done?"

We skidded to a halt behind him. Our throats tightened and our legs went numb at the fear in his voice.

Then we heard Michael's voice.

"Scott, stay right where you are."

Scott hesitated. He made a move to walk in, but

something made his hands go up and he backed up ever so slightly.

"Come on, Mike, don't do this."

Anna went to push past him.

"Anna!" Scott must have felt her coming. "He's got Rib Bone's gun. You and Rachel stay outside!"

We did what Scott told us to do. I heard Anna's voice quake as she spoke loudly, trying to persuade Scott to come out, trying to reason with Michael to put down the gun.

I stood next to the cave, resisting the urge to bolt in. I also had things I wanted to say. I wanted to tell Michael that someday things wouldn't seem so crazy. I wanted him to know that until that time, I would always be there. I wanted to tell him that he should know that, and he should care that I care, and because I cared it was only fair that he talk to me! I wanted to tell him to smarten up. But he didn't need me to tell him anything because he already had plenty of people telling him what he should do. So I stood and looked over the coulee, and for a very brief moment I felt how peaceful the world was. How quiet it was aside from their voices. How easy it was to watch the muddy South Saskatchewan River slide by. I started to cry.

"Let me come in and we'll talk." Scott's tone was desperate.

I heard a distinct click, a ratchet sound.

"I told you to go away."

I clutched my arms to my chest and shivered.

Anna stood next to me, also sniffing back tears. "I can see him in there. He's sitting in a chair with Rib Bone's gun across his lap."

"Anna, I think we'd better get Constable Rutledge. Michael's not thinking right. Scott shouldn't be trying to handle this on his own."

She wiped a tear from her cheek. "Not thinking right? Well, that's the understatement of the year."

Hearing a soft sound in the dirt behind us, we both jumped. Turning, we saw Rib Bone Squire leaning on his walking stick, climbing the last few feet to the cave. A wind lifted his white hair and blew out his cardigan. He stopped to catch his breath before speaking.

"I thought I might find you up here." Waving the cane toward the entrance, he raised the heavy skin of his forehead in a question.

We nodded. He then whispered something to Scott. He must have asked Michael's name.

"Michael," answered Scott.

Rib Bone patted him on the shoulder and told him to move outside. Scott tried to follow him in, but Rib Bone prevented him with his cane. He swept it across the entrance and pointed to the debris left behind when water swept through the cave the night before. "This cave is ready to give." And then he walked inside.

"Hey there, Michael," was all we heard him say.

"Mr. Squire, he has your gun," Scott shouted after him.

Rib Bone only raised his cane again, acknowledging

that he already knew this.

We never knew what passed between them. What was said by that crippled old man to Michael, who was also crippled, but in a very different way. But they were in there for nearly half an hour. Michael hadn't threatened or even shouted at Rib Bone. He was probably so shocked to see him, he didn't know what to say.

I caught a glimpse of them through the entrance. Michael sat with his elbow on an arm of the chair. He rested his head in his hand and his fingers were tangled in his curly black hair. His eyes were fixed on the muddy floor, and Rib Bone's gun lay across his lap. He looked exhausted, empty and broken. Rib Bone sat across from him, speaking gently, leaning forward, balancing his elbows on bony knees.

I sat on the ground next to Anna. We didn't talk. Instead we focused on trying to catch even a syllable of what was being said inside the cave. Scott paced further down by the path. I was sure he was also straining to hear the same thing. While we listened, Anna picked the tiny pink flowers off a cactus, slowly, crushing each one between her fingers. When they were gone, realizing what she'd done, she frowned at the ragged bits in the dirt and stared at her pink-stained hands.

Scott was the first to see the people coming. Constable Rutledge, Fire Chief Dunbar and Mr. Bell. They were followed by Mr. Potter and Mr. Brice and Uncle Colin, who carried his farm kit. Cory and Taylor and Simon pounded right behind them. And then there were the kids with the bright smears of paint on their faces. I heard Constable Rutledge tell them to, please, stay where they were. Many of them did, but not all.

"Is he in there?" Constable Rutledge asked once he had reached us. He struggled to catch his breath.

"Yes, but ..." Scott blocked the entrance to the cave.

"Get off of there!" the fire chief shouted at two kids who had scrambled on top of the cave to peer through the skylight. "This whole bank is ready to give."

They backed away.

They shouldn't have appeared as a crowd. It was just too much for Michael, as strung out and as volatile as he was. The sudden swarm of people, shouting, peering in at him. Not that they meant to harm him, but people should just know better than to gape in situations like that, because to Michael he was now some freakish curiosity, a part of the entertainment that day.

Mr. Bell made a move to pass by Scott.

Scott held up his arms to either side. "Mr. Squire is in there with him. I mean, it's quiet and they're talking."

But Mr. Bell ignored Scott, hustling him out of the way. "Michael! I'm right here, son."

For a withered old man who could hardly walk anymore, Rib Bone Squire was at the mouth of the cave in a flash. He stepped outside, guiding Mr. Bell with him. He urged everyone to give Michael time before they descended on him. He needed time and he needed to be alone.

Mr. Bell listened, but I don't think he heard a thing

because he ignored the suggestion, even though Constable Rutledge tried gently to hold him back. Frantically, he plowed forward to the cave again. He tried to control it, but his voice trembled as he shouted, "We're coming in now, Michael. Everything's going to be all right. Okay?"

He was answered by the thundering report of the shotgun.

And in the following few seconds, nothing on that prairie moved. Nothing but the dry wind and the silent shock of the blast, reverberating through the fragile walls of the cave. Seconds later we heard the thud of three beams as they fell from the ceiling to the floor. We heard the heavy dull sound of earth falling as the cave crumbled and collapsed into itself. The mouth of the cave vanished, and if Michael had called out for us, we hadn't heard.

For one small second we stood there in dumb confusion. Everyone was deathly quiet. Horrified. Someone began to softly cry. It was Mr. Bell who set the world in motion again.

"Oh, my god! Michael!" he screamed. He began to tear at the earth with his hands.

The people of Agatha began to tear at the earth with their hands, or with sticks or chunks of board retrieved from the fencing – whatever they could find. Rib Bone determined where we should dig, using his cane to point to the spot where Michael had been sitting. Mr. O'Connor tore back to his barn for tools to dig with, shovels and hoes. Every person who had come to search for Michael, including Anna and me, worked in a frenzy. Cory and Scott worked shoulder to shoulder, heaving earth, sweating, panting, sobbing as they dug into the sand. Taylor found a bucket to dig with. He paused for a moment as he looked over at me. It had once held red paint, and the stiff brush was stuck to the inside. He plucked out the brush, threw it aside and dug furiously.

Michael lay beneath one of the reinforcing beams. The beam had fallen at an angle and was supported at one end by the cattle trough. Lying a few inches beneath the end resting on the cattle trough, Michael's head had been protected from the impact of the falling earth, but his legs were pinned beneath the beam.

He lay crumpled and twisted, and although his eyes were open, he was not moving. Once the beam was lifted free, we could see that his legs were bent at impossible angles and there was little doubt that they were broken. Quickly kneeling next to him, Uncle Colin spoke quietly to him as he pulled a bag of fluid from his farm kit and, annoyed with his own broken arm for getting in the way, started an IV in Michael's arm. Michael was in shock and losing consciousness. His breathing was weak and his skin was gray.

Mr. Potter returned at a trot after finding two long, flat boards in the pile next to the fence. Mrs. O'Conner arrived with an armful of blankets, huffing and puffing after racing across the field. She lay one of the blankets across the boards, and Michael was lifted, gently and without changing his position, onto the makeshift stretcher. Uncle Colin ripped another blanket into two large pieces, one of which he rolled and placed between Michael's legs. The other piece he ripped into strips, which he used to secure Michael's lower body to the boards. Once this was done, Mrs. O'Conner covered him with the last blanket, bent down and brushed sand from his hair.

Chief Dunbar asked everyone to stay back and make room while they carried Michael up to O'Conner's farmhouse where the ambulance would meet them. Except Scott. Scott was allowed to go with them. I watched as he stumbled over the loose clumps of earth and across the railroad track toward O'Conner's farmhouse. He never once looked back at the cave.

Chief Dunbar shooed everyone away from the area and back to the exhibition grounds. Before we left, Anna and I walked over to where Rib Bone Squire was leaning quietly on his stick, inspecting the shotgun blast in the fallen beam.

"Mr. Squire," I reached out and took his hand, "thank you for whatever you said to Michael."

"I didn't say anything special," he told me. "He wanted to hear about Watson. Then I reminded him that all of you were waiting outside."

My foot hit something. Bending down, I picked up the empty paint bucket and with everything I had, I hurled it over the edge of the cliff.

FIFTEEN

I saw Michael one more time before I left Agatha. Uncle Colin drove me to the Medicine Hat Hospital. When I knocked on the door, Michael was lying on the hospital bed with both his legs in fresh white casts. He was watching an old movie.

"Hi," I said.

He turned toward me. His face was flushed and the hair around his temples was damp, like he'd just run a cross-country race or something. Like minutes before he'd been sprinting down the railroad track from the cave back to Agatha with the bright summer sun screaming at him the entire way.

"Hi," he said. He flicked off the television with the remote control.

"Mind if I come in for a bit?"

He struggled to sit higher in his bed. Pain skipped across his face, and so I wouldn't see it, he turned toward the window until he'd settled against his pillows again.

"Yeah, come in. I've been hoping you'd drop by sometime."

I walked into the room and sat next to him on a chair. I glanced up at the TV. "I hope I'm not interrupting anything."

Michael kind of grimaced. "Yeah, well, I was about to make a dash for the Coke machine in the lobby, but that can wait."

It was my turn to look away. I didn't want him to see my lip tremble, but it was impossible to stop the tears from spilling out. I wiped them away with the back of my hand.

"I meant I hoped I wasn't interrupting a good part of the movie. You know, like some really gruesome scene or something." I pulled a tissue from the box beside his bed and blew my nose.

Michael laughed a little. "No, you're not. Unfortunately there aren't any. Which is probably why it sucks so bad." He dropped the remote control on the crowded table beside him, next to an open box of chocolates. There was also a half-eaten submarine sandwich, an unopened bag of potato chips and a large basket of fruit competing for space. Next to that was a pile of old *Hot Rod* magazines. I looked around the room at the zillion flowers and other gifts Michael had received.

"My parents are here and I'm going home tomorrow," I told him. "I've come to say good-bye. I've come to make sure you're going to be okay." I had trouble looking at him so I looked at the chocolates instead. "Are you?"

Michael reached for the box of chocolates I was staring at. "Want a chocolate?"

"No, thanks."

"How about some chips? Or a grape?" He plucked one from the basket. "Look at the size of these things. They're like purple ping-pong balls." Frowning, he returned it to the basket. "But they're full of seeds."

I shook my head again. "No, thanks."

"Man, you're pretty hard to please. Okay, how about I order you the house special — a nice big bowl of sticky gray stew. I'd tell you what kind it is, but they boil it beyond recognition."

I laughed. "I really don't want anything. I just had lunch at Dot's. Anna insisted on taking me since it was our last time and everything. We had clubhouse sandwiches, although we actually ordered pizza, but," I shrugged, "you know how it is."

Michael smiled. "Yeah, I know exactly how it is."

He still hadn't answered my question. I looked down at my fingers spread across my knees. Silently, I asked again.

"Look, Rachel, before you go I want you to know that I'm really sorry about what happened. I'm sorry I flipped out and dragged you and Scott and Anna into it. I didn't mean to get you guys involved."

"You didn't drag us into it. We wouldn't have let

you go through it alone."

Michael looked at me. I hoped he knew that what I said was true. He took a deep breath, folded his hands over his stomach and lay still.

"Will you tell me what happened?"

I was immediately sorry I'd asked, because he frowned and turned toward the window. But maybe remembering that I was leaving and maybe thinking that I deserved an explanation, he turned back.

"All right."

And he told me what happened the night before the cave collapsed.

He was going down to the cave one last time and then he was going to take off. Hitchhike to the west coast. Get out of Agatha. He knew they'd be after him soon, if not already, for destroying Taylor's car. He was scared. He'd done things and he didn't know why and he didn't recognize himself anymore. And he didn't know how to go back.

The weather turned dismal that night after he left me. It was raining hard by the time he'd passed the exhibition grounds and so black he could barely tell the sky from the ground. Only a very dull moon lit his way along the railroad track, and it was a mud slide down to the cave, down the slope from O'Conner's field. Michael skated down it, but ten feet from the mouth of the cave he had to stop. It was as far as he could go. He stood outside, listening to the water pour through the skylight. He watched as the mud ran over his shoes and slopped over the edge of the cliff. He knew it was only a matter of time before the cave would disappear entirely.

And as he stood in the rain and the minutes passed and the pieces of his world washed by, he saw himself going with it. He saw himself plunging into Buffalo Coulee, spinning down the river, as out of control as a bloated cow. He saw his body roaring along, bumping against the bank, collecting deadwood. Suddenly – absolutely – he knew he didn't want to go with it. He didn't want to be pulled from the river a week later by horrified kids. He didn't want to be a statistic. An example. He didn't want to be like Nick and just disappear.

He panicked. He ran down the railroad track, across the train trestle and up the hill to the shed behind Rib Bone's cabin. He sat in Rib Bone's old Chevy, cold and wet and confused. During the night the rain stopped, and by dawn the sun glowed rose in the sky. It was when he saw Rib Bone pulling thistles in his garden that he went into his cabin and stole the shotgun.

"I don't even know why I took it. Except that I knew what I'd done and how much trouble I was in. I guess I thought they'd be coming after me with their guns blazing." Michael stopped talking. Then he said, "I only fired at the beam to stop them from coming in."

"Yes," I said. "I know."

I didn't stay much longer. Michael claimed he was not tired, but he was pale now, and besides, I had to get back to Uncle Colin's and pack. I warned him I was going to harass him. "I'm going to write to you, and I won't stop writing to you until you write back and let me know what's going on in your life."

He laughed, but he promised that he would. I hugged him carefully and kissed his forehead. I said good-bye and turned to go.

"Rach?"

"Yeah?"

"Something else I'm sorry about. I'm sorry about us. I'm sorry all this got in the way."

I smiled. "That's okay. Hey, maybe if I come back we can start over again?"

"Naw, let's start from where we left off."

I nodded.

It was when he raised his arm to wave at me as I stood in the doorway that I caught the flash of Nick's watch.

"It's okay?" I said, pointing to it, knowing he was wearing it when the cave fell in.

"It's okay," he said. "It's amazingly shock resistant. Nick would have been impressed."

I agreed.

■ ■ ■

That night, Uncle Colin and Aunt Sandy had a good-bye party for me at their house. I don't really even want to talk about it because I just blubbered most of the night anyway. I even had trouble saying good-bye to Cory and Taylor.

When I thanked Uncle Colin and Aunt Sandy the next morning for having me, they invited me to come back again next summer.

"You have to come back," Uncle Colin told me, winking. "I haven't shown you how to extract a horse's tooth."

I winked back. "I'll look forward to it." I wondered that he didn't have more broken bones.

■ ■ ■

It's a cold gloomy November day and the branches of the rhododendron outside my window look saggy and sad after six weeks of rain. I'm sitting at the computer, swinging in the swivel chair, looking out the window at the freighters in Burrard Inlet and missing Sean. This is the kind of Sunday afternoon we used to do things together. We'd go to A & B Sound or we'd strike a deal — he'd hang around the mall waiting for me while I looked for shoes, if I'd wait for him while he admired the saxophones in the music store one more time.

I just got an e-mail from Anna. I e-mail her and Michael and Scott all the time. She's really looking forward to coming out to Vancouver and staying with me during the Christmas break. And she tells me that Michael is getting better every day.

Dad sticks his head in the room. "Hey, what are you up to?"

"Just talking to Anna," I tell him.

"How's she doing? Have they managed to keep the clinic running without you?"

Dad has settled down a lot in the last two months, ever since business picked up where he works and they were able to hire another engineer. He hasn't been nearly as negative about who I'm hanging around with and he sometimes even listens to what I say. I've forgiven him for being so difficult in the past few months. I've put it down to a phase.

"She's really looking forward to coming out at Christmas."

He nods. "Well, tell her we're looking forward to having her. And Michael? How is he?"

I tell him everything I know about Michael. I mean, within reason. I figure since Dad is making an effort to listen, I may as well make the effort to talk. In fact, just to see him smile the other day I told him he was right about Troy Atkinson. But I also told him that talking and listening — it works both ways.

"I'm glad to hear he's recovering," he says when I'm finished. He pauses before closing the door. "Make sure Michael knows he's welcome to come out and spend some time with us whenever he likes."

"Thanks, Dad. I'll let him know."

I finish reading Anna's email. Michael is still on crutches, but that doesn't stop him from whipping down the halls ahead of everyone else. She wonders if he and Scott have somehow customized his crutches, added some kind of springs to the joints or special tips to the bottom or whatever to make them go faster.

I smile. No doubt.

She also tells me that Michael received a suspended sentence for drowning Taylor's limousine. He's going to counseling and he was assigned to do community service, for which Rib Bone volunteered. He had an old car in his shed that needed some work, he told the circuit judge. He could really use a hand to get it running again; he was getting too old to make the long walk into town.

I reach for the letter I received from Michael two days ago. The one in which he tells me all of this himself. Leaning back in my chair, I look out the window and watch the big drops of rain splash against the branches of the rhododendrons. One after another they come down, beating against the leaves. Each time one hits, a leaf bends just a little bit lower. The water rolls off and the weight is gone and the leaf bounces up again. But never quite so high as it was before.

I read the letter again and I think about last summer in Agatha and Michael. And I still wonder how we had all missed the signs.

But he's going to be all right. I can see Michael with Rib Bone Squire by his side. I am standing outside the exhibition grounds watching the two of them, supported by their walking sticks, hobble down the railroad tracks on their way to Buffalo Coulee. The sun is hot and the sky is blue and the flat yellow land stretches hundreds of miles into the distance, to the Sweet Grass Hills of Montana.

Rib Bone appears to hear something. He stops and looks around. Lifting his cane, he points to a meadowlark, singing from where it's perched on a long blade of prairie grass. Rib Bone stumbles a bit. Michael catches him by the arm and together they go on.

Praise for Katherine Holubitsky's first novel,
ALONE AT NINETY FOOT

"... this novel feels authentic and insightful ..."
- *Publishers Weekly*

"... a moving, sometimes funny story of recovery."
- *Quill & Quire*

"... this is good, this is really good. Holubitsky draws the characters with the confidence and authenticity of a writer in tune with today's teens."
- *Julie Johnston*

Awards and Citations:

★ Young Adult Book of the Year Award - Canadian Library Association

★ IODE Violet Downey Book Award

★ Best Books for Young Adults — American Library Association

★ Pick of the Lists — American Booksellers Association

★ New York Public Library Books for the Teen Age

★ Best Books for Young Adults — Teacher Librarian Magazine

★ Our Choice — starred selection — Canadian Children's Book Centre